OLDE TUDOR

A ghost story
by
David Ralph Williams

Cursed be he that moves my bones

William Shakespeare

That darksome cave they enter, where they find
that cursed man, low sitting on the ground,
musing full sadly in his sullein mind.

Edmund Spenser

This book is dedicated to the following people, my parents Hilda and Ralph, my wife Leesa and children (Luke, Katie and Hannah.) My partner in crime (ghost hunting and writing) The Baron Templar (A.K.A Michael McManus), John Williams my first reader of stories created during long ago summers on coffee tables in front rooms.

I know not what this creature is, or from whence it came. But it would appear to have my scent, and a desire to instil fear in my heart and soul. What it wants, I can only guess.

(Taken from - An archaeological study of Thornbarrow Cavern - by the Reverend George Charles Redgrave (Saint Peter's Parish Church)

1

Arthur Brierly entered the door to his son, Jacob's office. Arthur was wearing his overcoat, hat, and was in a jolly mood, not unusual for the senior Brierly. "Jack, how about we go into the town for a spot of lunch, I rather fancy the beef and ale pie at the Red Heart Inn. Can I tempt you?" Jacob had just finished adding a shovel of coal to the fire grate that stood on the far wall adjacent to his desk. He took out a fob watch from his waistcoat pocket and glanced at it.

"I am thoroughly tempted father, unfortunately I have an appointment with a client at any moment," spoke Jacob in disappointment.

"I've told you before lad, always keep the lunch hour free. Oh Bish! Can you not make an excuse and cancel?"

"I best not Father. You go on ahead, when I'm finished I will follow you over." Jacob became aware of a noise outside the office of Brierly and Son, Property Agents. He walked over to the large bay window and saw a mature gentleman sporting a thick tweed jacket and brown trilby leaning his bicycle against the front of the offices before entering the main door. "He's here, I think."

"Alright, I'll leave you to it. Don't be long. I could do with some company today if you must know, been stuck in my stuffy office all morning," said Arthur Brierly.

The door to Jacob's office opened and the gentleman in the tweed jacket entered. Arthur tipped his hat and mumbled, "good day," before leaving his son to deal with him. The man walked over to Jacob who now stood behind his desk. He offered his hand to Jacob.

"Alistair Swift, we have an appointment I believe?" Jacob shook Alistair's hand warmly.

"We do indeed Mister Swift, please take a seat," Jacob said indicating the only other seat in the room. Alistair drew the chair closer to Jacob's desk, he glanced over at the fire that was now crackling into life, bright yellow flames licked across the fresh black coal cobbles.

"Splendid fire. It's rather chilly outside today. Would you mind if I warm myself near to it?"

"Of course, please do. I noticed you came on a bicycle, you must be frozen!" added Jacob.

"I never learned to drive, but it's the hands you see, the cold metal of the handlebars. Chills the fingers to the bone." Alistair rose from his seat and pushed his hands towards the warm fire rubbing them together. Jacob was busy retrieving a paper file from his desk drawer. He opened the file.

"Mister Swift, I recollect from our telephone conversation the other week that you are seeking a property close to the town, and you were quite precise as to your specifications. You are looking for a property with character is that right?" Jacob continued to read over the collection of papers he had removed from the file.

"Yes, that's right, I can't abide those modern houses. I always thought I'd like a house with some history associated," said Alistair now reseating himself at Jacob's desk.

"Well, I have a selection for you to look at," Jacob said and handed him the stack of papers. Alistair studied each sheet. There were details of a variety of properties, some had sketches associated whilst a few of them had monochrome photographs attached. None of the houses seemed to spark an interest in Alistair.

"They are all very nice, but not quite what I'm after I'm afraid," Alistair said and handed the papers back to Jacob.

"The problem is, Thornbarrow is only a small town, a village really. Not a great deal of choice."

"Yes, I do understand. But I want my purchase to be just right, and I do rather like the town."

"Have you considered renting?" Jacob asked.

"Well, I have recently retired from my profession, teaching. I was a teacher at a boy's school, not far from here. I taught at the school for almost twenty-eight years! The teaching post came with its own accommodation. So, you see, I really much would like to finally own my own home. You understand?"

"Of course. A teacher you say," Jacob placed the papers back in the file leaving it on the desk top.

"Yes, I taught history, with a little mathematics," spoke Alistair proudly.

"A man with his feet firmly on the ground. Not open to fanciful leanings I would presume?" said Jacob who now rose from behind his desk and walked over to a small oak cupboard in the corner of the office. He appeared to hesitate and ponder for a moment before he opened the cupboard and brought out a large cardboard box.

"Yes, you could say so. I also rather fancy myself as a bit of an amateur artist. I must fill up my time with something you understand. It's such a shock to the system leaving ones employ."

"Yes, I can imagine." Jacob re-seated himself behind his desk. "Mister Swift, I do have one property you might be interested in. We have had it on our books for a considerable time. It has become a little dilapidated, and the grounds on which it stands are somewhat overgrown. However, I'm sure it will satisfy some of your stipulations." Jacob opened the box and removed some dusty folded papers. He handed them to Alistair. "There are no photographs I'm afraid, just the sketches that come with the documents." Alistair examined the papers, the property had a name, Olde Tudor.

Alistair sat quietly and read through the details. There were two pen and ink sketches, one showed an aerial map with the position of the house relative to the fields and tracks situated nearby. The other was a sketch of the front aspect of the house. It depicted a Tudor style house, with eaves, exposed wooden frames between wattle and daub, a tall chimney and a thatched roof. Alistair's face beamed.

"This is exactly right. Just what I hoped I'd find," he sang merrily.

"Like I said, the sketches are a little misleading, it's not as tidy now you understand. The building I believe is generally sound. The thatch was replaced by the family that owns it a few years back in forty-two. It has a tiled roof now. A more practical solution I think."

"Indeed. I would like to see this property. Do you have time today?" Alistair asked hopefully. Jacob glanced at the clock that perched atop the mantle. He winced as his mind wandered to the promise of a meal that awaited at the Red Hart. This nourishment seemed now to be a diminishing prospect.

"Of course. I can take you there now if you have the time. It's not such a long walk from the town."

"That would be splendid, thank you." Alistair rose from his seat and waited for Jacob to don his hat and coat.

******

Jacob Brierly and Alistair Swift were walking with a good pace. It was a chilly November day. The cobbled streets were particularly treacherous when covered in such a coating of icy frost that had yet to melt. The road they were both on, the main route out of Thornbarrow, took a steep decline after crossing the perimeter of the centre of town. The road eventually narrowed to become a single dirt track that was laden with pot holes and dips, all of which were filled with iced rainwater.

Alistair was walking with his bicycle, holding the handlebars. The steep decline of the track and the hard, glassy feel underfoot made the walk a rather difficult one. Eventually after a good twenty minutes, they reached the bottom of the hill. The road forked into two further single dirt tracks, equally as slippery and frozen as the parent track that they branched from. Jacob Brierly stopped at the fork in the road. "I believe it's the left track we need to take Mister Swift," he said and he took the lead. Alistair carefully followed, wheeling his bicycle and avoiding the frozen tractor tyre furrows that crossed from field onto road.

About a quarter of a mile down the track a clump of trees and overgrown bushes came into view. "That's the place, up ahead. It's the only property on this road for at least five miles," said Jacob. They both continued towards the huddle of skeletal trees, each with only a few remaining golden leaves still clinging to lichen encrusted twig in a desperate attempt to defy the recent fall. When they reached the house, Alistair leaned his bicycle against the stone wall at the front, most of which was covered in trailing ivy.

There was a small yet robust iron gate that wasn't locked. Jacob pushed the gate and it swung inwards. Both men treaded a meandering red brick pathway that led up to the front porch. "Like I said," started Jacob, "it's a little overgrown, but nothing a good gardener couldn't put to rights." Alistair stood hands on hips taking in the house's full aspect.

"It's just as I hoped it would be. Marvellous," he said. Jacob removed a long black key from an envelope that was inside a thin satchel he was carrying. He inserted the key into the lock on the door and twisted.

"The gardens to this house have some rather interesting quirks that I'm sure you will appreciate, but first let's go inside as you will see there remains a lot of the original furniture." Jacob finished as he stepped inside the hallway.

Once inside, the door was closed to keep out the bitter cold. Both men walked through the hall and along a short corridor before they reached the main reception room.

It was clear to Alistair that the house had remained locked up and empty for a considerable amount of time. Thick sheets of cobwebs hung from the light fittings on the ceiling. The floor was mostly stone flagging or wood planks, but there were a few rugs that were heavily soiled with a mixture of dirt and dust. The dust Alistair observed was at the least, half an inch thick where it covered shelving and the assortment of old oak furniture. In the centre of the room stood a grand open fireplace with a thick iron burning grate and basket within.

Jacob continued to lead the way through the rest of the house which comprised of a large kitchen complete with stove and impressive bulky dining table. There were an assortment of pots and pans, mostly fashioned from copper and arranged on a series of shelves on the back wall. Alistair still had a smile on his face as they walked from room to room.

Eventually they examined the master bedroom. There was another smaller bedroom that was connected to the master room via a small narrow corridor. The master bedroom contained a large oak bedstead with high panelled headboard. The layering of dust upon the carved embellishments of the headboard seemed to pick out and highlight each chiselled mark and groove that had been produced so long ago by the carpenter who created the remarkable article. "Only two bedrooms I'm afraid, and the smaller one is a little cramped," explained Jacob.

"It's more than I need, I'm not married you see, and I don't have any relatives that I imagine would be thinking about staying here," said Alistair, "I was engaged once, a long while ago now, but then the war happened. The town in which she lived was heavily bombed. I lost her, you see."

"I'm terribly sorry to hear that Mister Swift I really am."

"Oh, thank you. But I imagine many people have loved and lost, and have a similar story as I. The Nazi menace cast a terrible shadow over millions of lives. I happen to be just one."

Alistair crossed over to the bedroom window. The small diamond shaped leaded window panes were somewhat begrimed and he had to remove a handkerchief from his pocket to wipe them clean before he could view the garden below. "I'd very much like to see outside now if I may. You mentioned quirks?"

"Yes, I think you'll be quite surprised." Jacob descended the stairs that led back down to the lower house with Alistair following.

The gardens were quite large and they were very overgrown by nettle and a myriad of knotty and prickly creeper. Jacob used an old branch that had fallen from a large ash tree to beat down the nettles allowing them to make a path across what was once a long lawn.

The first structure they came across was an old brick built workshop. Jacob fished out another key from his satchel and opened the door. "As you can see, quite a large outbuilding, and fully tooled." Alistair examined some of the tools that were haphazardly scattered across both large work benches.

There were racks of hammers, saws, screwdrivers and other assorted tools all fastened to hooks. There was a large vice fixed to the larger of the two work benches. He noticed that the windows to the workshop were still taped up to prevent the occupant from being injured by shattered glass during an air raid.

"Yes, plenty to tinker around with. I am astonished that all this stuff has been left here along with the furniture at the house. Does it all come with the sale?" asked Alistair.

"Yes, I believe it does. The family who still own the property have no use for it."

"Do they still live within Thornbarrow?"

"No, they moved to London, just after the war. It was their great uncle who owned the house, a Mister. . . Redgrave, George Redgrave. The old Parson I believe." Jacob motioned for them both to leave the workshop and continue to explore the garden.

A short walk from the workshop brought them both to a huge standing stone. Alistair took off his hat and shielded his eyes from the low dazzling winter sun so that he could view the edifice. "I say, is that what I think it is?" he said astounded.

"It's a monolith. The last of a series of standing stones I believe. Most were broken up a century or so since and used to construct some of the houses in the village along with the local church. This one survived. The last stone of Thornbarrow." Alistair walked over to touch the stone. It was huge, at least two and a half times the height and width of him.

"A monolithic stone. And it stands on the land with the house?"

"Yes, if you were to purchase this house you would also be the owner of the monolith." Alistair was astounded at this news.

"Surely something like this has such immense historical value. It can't be right that I could simply own it."

"Well, it is listed as part of the deeds to this property. Nobody really seems to care Mister Swift. The previous owners of the house have all become, how should I say. . . custodians of the monolith if you like."

"I see. Well I have to say, you have taken my breath away Mister Brierly, you really have!"

"And there is one more surprise Mister Swift. Follow me please," said Jacob as he led a path behind the monolith to a small outcrop of rock that jutted up and out of the ground. The rocks were partially covered by the prickly creepers of a wild black berry bush. Alistair studied the rocky protrusion which seemed to be totally out of place in its surroundings.

"I say, what on earth is the purpose of this structure? It's not an ice house, is it?" Alistair asked.

"No, but I dare say it could be used as one. It's a cave Mister Swift."

"A cave? Am I hearing you correctly?"

"Indeed you are. According to the deeds, this is listed as a cavern, and runs quite deep underground. It's a natural cavern formed by glaciers I think. I expect you would know about these things being a teacher Mister Swift?"

"Indeed. A cave. I can hardly believe it. And this also comes with the house and grounds, like the monolith?"

"It does." Alistair chuckled to himself as he made his way over to examine the structure. The apparent entrance to the cavern was barred by a heavy wrought iron gate that was locked with a formidable looking padlock.

"Why is it locked? Do you have the key?" Jacob searched through his satchel, there were only the keys to the house and workshop.

"I'm afraid I don't Mister Swift. I can ask the owners, they might have it, otherwise it may be around someplace. Perhaps in the workshop." Alistair rattled the gate.

"Seems such a secure gate. I wonder what possessed them to seal it off so thoroughly?"

"Perhaps it was dangerous. A rockfall maybe?"

"Yes perhaps that was it. Still, I would very much like to explore down there wouldn't you?"

"I'm not sure that I would. I get a bit claustrophobic you see!" Jacob and Alistair walked back through the overgrown gardens until they found themselves standing on the brick path that led back up to the house.

"I am very impressed with the house Mister Brierly. I think I would rather like to make an offer. What is the asking price exactly?" Jacob pulled out a document from his satchel and read it over.

"Four thousand, nine hundred and fifty pounds. But I expect they are open to offers."

"I would like to offer the asking price. Would you be able to speak with the owner and discuss all the particulars?"

"Of course. I will make a telephone call back at the office. Are you staying locally Mister Swift?"

"Yes, I have a room at the Red Hart Inn, in the centre of town."

"Good, I will contact you later. Hopefully with some good news," Jacob replied happy to have such an enthusiastic client.

"I hope so Mister Brierly, I am quite taken with the old place. I can see myself being very happy here. Yes, very happy."

2

It was a bitter January day. Alistair Richard Swift had travelled by train from Cromer to Thornbarrow. He had been staying with his sister, Gwen whilst the house sale of Olde Tudor progressed. Finally deeds to the property were exchanged and he had organised delivery of his possessions from temporary storage at his sister's house to Olde Tudor.

Alistair had taken a taxi from the station to the house. On arrival, he was greeted by the sight of a small lorry parked outside his new home and blocking the road. Alistair paid the cabbie his tariff then he walked over to the lorry. The wind was getting up and it had a particularly savage bite to it. The first flurries of snow had started to fall.

The driver of the lorry was leaning against the vehicle whilst he refilled his pipe with tobacco. "Good day, I hope you haven't been waiting long," apologised Alistair. The driver tipped his cap and finished lighting his pipe before he answered.

"No Squire, been 'ere no longer than twenty or so minutes."

"That's good. The weather is starting to decline I fear," the driver cast a glance up at the leaden sky.

"I think there's a lot of snow up there Squire, bout ready to drop, I'd say." Alistair tilted his head in time for a large flat snowflake to melt on his eyeball.

"I think you're right about that! I'm just waiting for the agent to arrive with the keys, he shouldn't be long." As Alistair finished both he and the driver became aware of the sound of a motor engine just around the bend in the road. They both stood in the road to see if it was the agent and were relieved to see a green Triumph Roadster approach them. Alistair recognised the driver to be Jacob Brierly. Jacob tooted his horn before stopping just behind the lorry. Alistair walked over to greet him.

"Good afternoon," he said and Jacob climbed out of his car and shook his hand warmly.

"Good afternoon Mister Swift. Your possessions are here too I see!" he said pointing to the lorry. The driver had used his fist to bang on the passenger side of the lorry and another man climbed down and helped him to untie the tarpaulin that covered two large tea chests, and a mattress.

"Yes, not an awful lot. Living in one room at the boy's school for all those years, I just didn't amass much in the way of articles and furniture. Shouldn't take them that long to get it all inside."

"Well, in this weather that's a good thing," Jacob said and he opened his satchel and handed Alistair a keyring. "There are two keys to the front of the house but only one to the back, so you might want to have another one cut. There's also the key to the workshop." Alistair thanked Jacob as he studied the keys.

"Oh, did you manage to find the key to that padlock on the gate to the cave?" Alistair asked.

"No, sorry. I did ask the vender, but they said they were never handed any gate key when they came into possession of the house following the death of the previous owner," explained Jacob.

"Oh, that's a shame. Never mind, I can always find a way around that at some point. Right now I need to settle inside, get a fire on."

"Yes indeed Mister Swift, I hear the weather is turning bitterly cold for the next few days, and the sky looks full of snow. I did manage to get the electricity reconnected in advance of your arrival."

"Thank you so much for that, I wasn't expecting everything done, you see I brought a lot of candles." Alistair reached into the pocket of his overcoat and brought out a handful of candles for Jacob to see."

"There's also a wood shed well stocked, it's at the back of the workshop."

"Good! Well I shouldn't be in need of anything for the time being. I managed to pick up a few groceries from a shop on the station, milk, eggs, bread, tea. That kind of thing," remarked Alistair.

The tea chests had been unloaded into the road. The two delivery men asked Alistair where he wanted them moving to. He told them to take them straight through to the main reception room. He trotted up to the main door and opened it wide, propping it open with a loose brick he found on the floor near the doorstep.

Each crate was carefully carried into the house. Alistair paid the two men and gave them a respectable tip. Jacob Brierly wished Alistair good luck with his new home and quickly climbed back into his car to move it out of the way of the lorry so it could reverse and carry out an awkward turn and be driven back up the hill into the town. Jacob tooted his car horn again as he also departed back for the town. Rubbing his chilled hands together Alistair made his way inside Olde Tudor.

******

With his bed made, the final crate emptied, and the articles within all placed into appropriate places, Alistair set about a spot of cleaning up. First he dusted all the furniture using a small soft hand brush he had found in a kitchen cupboard. Then he swept the floor several times until he was satisfied he had removed most of the dust and dirt that had settled there during the house's period of abandonment.

The wind had picked up considerably. One raging bluster after another pushed against the house, rattling the delicate windows. Occasionally the lights flickered during the loudest gusts. Alistair decided that he would place candles around the house keeping one or two lit just in case the storm caused a power outage. With the unpacking completed and the house cleaned to an acceptable level, Alistair decided he would get a fire lit so he set off in search of some fuel.

The night was drawing in fast. Alistair used a small torch he had packed into one of the crates to go in search of the wood shed. He found the shed and indeed it was well stocked as Jacob had said with dried seasoned firewood. It had probably been sitting there for a few years he thought. A lot of it even had woodworm.

Inside the shed was a large wicker basket. He filled the basket with enough wood to last the evening. He also saw a hurricane lamp hanging from a rusty nail. He unhooked it and gave it a shake. There appeared to be enough paraffin in the reservoir. He thought the lamp was a good discovery, especially in wind as strong as this tonight. He placed the lamp into the basket. He then saw a stack of old newspapers and magazines. He scooped up a handful and tucked them underneath his arm. He gripped the basket and left the shed.

About half way back to the front of the house he heard a rattling noise. At first the wind was so strong and loud he thought he'd imagined it, but as the latest gusts died down momentarily, he heard it again. Placing the basket down and resting a loose brick on top of the stack of papers he walked around the back of the house following the noise.

Moving his arm slowly, the weak iridescent beam of light from his torch first picked out the monolith. The grass at its base was thrashing wildly against the lichen encrusted stone. The sound of rattling persisted further. Turning away from the monolith, the torchlight picked out the shape of the cavern rocks. Alistair was a little perturbed to realise that the rattling seemed to be emanating from this feature.

Slowly he walked over towards the cave entrance. The wrought iron gate that sealed the mouth of the cave was shaking in the wind. Relieved that he had discovered the source of the disturbing noise he turned to walk back to the house when he was startled by a dark shape that darted past his legs.

Dropping the torch in fright he let out a brief shriek before collecting himself together and calming down. He was self-critical of his response to what he now saw to be a cat, and he cursed his foolishness. Probably a stray he thought on account that his was the only house for five miles according to Jacob Brierly. After a brief search on the ground, he picked up the torch. The front end that housed the bulb had shattered. He tossed the now useless implement onto the grass.

On his way back to the front of the house he was followed by the cat that rubbed against his legs as he retrieved the wood basket and papers. "So you want to come inside do you? Well I suppose you can, if you have no other place to go," Alistair said, talking to the cat as it sauntered inside the front door.

The cat continued to rub and purr against Alistair as he started to lay a fire. He tore pages of newspaper and twisted them to form a paper nest in the grate. Underneath the first newspaper was an odd leather bound book. He examined it briefly with curiosity and then placed the book on top of the mantelpiece so that he could peruse it later.

Next he arranged some smaller pieces of wood on top of the paper in a pyramid and then lit the paper beneath using a match. Once the paper and kindling had caught the fire he lifted two medium sized wood logs from the basket and placed them carefully on top of the other burning wood. Satisfied with his fire building efforts, Alistair sat himself down on one of two fireside chairs that had come with the purchase of the house.

The sleek grey moggy jumped onto Alistair's lap and continued to purr loudly. "Friendly cat, aren't you," he said as he began to stroke the slate grey soft fur. "Do you have a name my little friend, eh? If only I knew your name. Maybe you don't have a name, is that it?" the cat only continued to purr. "Well, because I don't know who you are, I shall call you Smokey, because your fur being as grey as the smoke that now travels up the chimney of this old house!" chuckled Alistair. "Now Smokey, how about a little supper eh?"

In the kitchen Alistair prepared a meal consisting of tinned pilchards and bread and butter for himself, and just pilchards for Smokey. He was just about to bring their supper through to the main drawing room when the electricity was suddenly cut off. The house was plunged into darkness. Placing down the food on the large dining table, he quickly went through to the drawing room and began to light the candles he had prepared earlier for such an eventuality. Damn the wind, he thought.

Once the house had sufficient light, he brought through the supper he'd prepared. He set

Smokey's pilchards down next to the hearth; Smokey gobbled them up greedily. Walking over to the front window, Alistair peered outside. Branches of the large ash tree were bending by the force of the wind, that seemed to be growing even stronger. The heavens had finally decided to release their cargo of snow, and it was settling fast. Alistair feared snow drifts due to the wind, but as there was nothing he could do about it he closed the old mottled curtains and settled down to eat his supper.

After his meal, Alistair decided to try and call the electricity board. He lifted the receiver on the black Bakelite telephone that was connected in the hallway, then used the rotary dial to call an operator. When he placed the receiver to his ear he couldn't hear any dial tone. He realised that the storm had apparently knocked out his phone line as well as his electricity supply. He made his way back to the drawing room to tell Smokey. He had nobody else to share the bad news with.

Alistair had eventually settled himself in bed. He had brought with him the curious leather covered book he had found mixed amongst the old newspapers and magazines in the wood shed. Smokey was curled up on the end of the bed. Alistair wondered how many people had slept in the bed he now occupied, it was quite a stately bed and he guessed it to be dating from the seventeenth century, or maybe even earlier.

A candle burned on a bedside table; the light was adequate to enable the reading of a book. The wind continued to rush against the bedroom window, finding its way inside through gaps where the leaded light cement had decayed and crumbled and dropped from some of the individual glass panes. Sometimes the threadbare curtain covering the window would billow distracting Alistair from his reading. Alistair began to flick through the pages of the book. It was a hand-written journal or study. The musty scent from its pages seemed to give off a trace of the soul of the person who wrote in it. The first words he read – *An archaeological study of Thornbarrow Cavern, by the Reverend George Charles Redgrave (Saint Peter's Parish Church).* There was a passage that spoke about some of the history of the cavern. Alistair found this to be most interesting.

History of Thornbarrow cavern:

The Cave was certainly used as a place of temporary shelter from the elements of nature. Possibly also for storing produce and meat and as refuge from criminal activity or war between neighbouring groups or tribes. Curiosity probably drove many prehistoric explorers to enter caves seeking answers to many questions concerning their length, depth, and extent and to what might be hidden inside. However, it is possible that the first few meters of the entrance to the cave, the area where sunlight would reach, might have been permanently inhabited.

The cave has splendid examples of Palaeolithic paintings. Close to twenty paintings, mostly of animals, decorate the interior walls of the cave in impressive compositions. Horses are the most numerous, but deer, birds, and even some human forms can also be found. The art probably dates from c. 17,000 to c. 15,000 BCE.

The art was created by the skilled hands of humans living in the area at that time. the artists used complex methods to create their paintings, using minerals as pigments for their images. The predominant colours appear to be red, yellow and black. Red was provided by hematite, either raw or as found within red clay. Yellow by iron oxyhydroxides, and black either by charcoal or manganese oxides.

The pigments were most probably prepared by grinding, mixing, or even heating. Following the preparatory process, they were then transferred onto the cave walls. Painting techniques included drawing with fingers or charcoal, then applying the pigment with primitive kinds of brushes probably made of hair or moss. Some pigment has obviously been applied by blowing the pigment on a stencil or directly onto the wall with, for instance, a hollow bone.

After using a paraffin lamp to light my way further along the cavern I discovered a variety of animal bones and flint and stone tools. Many of the tools I brought back to the house in order to make the sketches found in this book.

After further exploration, I discovered some neat piles of rocks under which I discovered the bones of three hominids. One male, one female (adult), and one female (child). I believe them to be a family.

The remains were difficult to study due to the bones being broken up quite badly. The skulls were also damaged. I believe all three had been killed as part of some prehistoric ritual sacrifice.

The next few pages in the book were dedicated to the author's sketches of an assortment of stone tools that were discovered. The illustrations were done in pencil and ink and Alistair was impressed by the draughtsmanship skills of the author. Each stone and flint implement was labelled as to its supposed function, material it was constructed from, and precisely where it was discovered in the cave. Each object was given a unique identifying number.

Alistair's eyes were growing heavy. He skipped past the lengthy sketches and discovered that a collection of pages that followed had been crudely ripped from the book. This surprised him as the author had been so careful, so meticulous prior to this event. Perhaps, he thought, that someone had actually used the pages to start a fire. What an awful thing to do when there was a stack of alternative papers in the shed.

The first remaining unspoiled page that followed the scraps of torn pages had something written in scrappy handwriting. It was the same handwriting of the author, but less neat. There was an urgency about it. It simply said – *I should have left the dead to rest in peace, my selfish prying, and intrusive curiosity has brought nothing but malignity upon me.*

On the following page, there seemed to be a prayer, written down in the same urgent handwriting:

I run to you, Lord,
for protection.
So come to my rescue.
Listen to my prayer
and keep me safe.
Be my mighty rock,
the place
where I can always run
for protection.

You made me suffer a lot,
but you will bring me
back from this deep pit
and take my sorrow away.

The wind continued to moan throughout the night. It kept Alistair awake, but so did something else. The relentless shaking and rattling of the cavern gate as it became a plaything of the wind's airy fingers. As he lay awake trying to entice sleep, he decided that he would attempt to break through the padlock in the morning. There surely must be adequate tools in the workshop he thought. And when he had the gate open he intended to explore the cave. The journal written by the Reverend George Charles Redgrave had wet his appetite for adventure.

3

Alistair awoke the next morning feeling eager to get outside and to poke around the various outbuildings, to see what he could discover. Most of all he wanted to get the gate to the cave opened.

Before he ventured outside he cleaned the ash from the fire grate and he lay a new fire ready for the night ahead. He also set about getting the oven stoked with kindling; he didn't fancy another cold supper of tinned pilchards. When he was finished with his morning chores, the last of which was to pour a saucer of milk for his newly acquired cat, he wrapped himself up in a thick woollen sweater, overcoat, and scarf before stepping outside.

The snow flurries had died away during the night, replaced with sleet and icy rain. The sky however told him that the worst of the weather was yet to come. The first thing Alistair did was to stock up on logs from out of the wood shed. He piled them high just inside of the back door as he didn't fancy another trek around the garden in the dark. His next mission was to peruse what tools and other implements had been left in the workshop.

The workshop was cold and damp inside. The small windows created a gloomy interior. He found another hurricane lamp and also a canister of paraffin. He filled the lamp and lit the wick using matches that were left on a shelf above a large vice. The lamp provided sufficient illumination for him to look around.

Most of the tools seemed to be scattered about rather haphazardly. Alistair surmised that somebody had rummaged about through the tools, probably the seller of the property. He guessed they were looking for any useful tools they could take away before the sale went through.

He walked up to a rack that had an array of wood saws, and hacksaws. There were gaps to suggest that some of the better tools had been removed. He unhooked an old looking hacksaw, the main body of the tool had rusted but it still looked sturdy enough.

Under the main bench a small wooden crate, the type used to store apples caught his eye. Placing the hacksaw down on the bench he crouched low so that he could pull the crate out towards him. It was heavy.

The crate contained an assortment of what he first thought were rocks surrounded with dry straw for packing. Upon closer examination, he realised that they were stone tools. A wave of excitement flowed through him as he handled the razor-sharp flints. He realised that these were the objects that had been recovered from the cave and the subject of the many illustrations in the journal.

The crate was packed full of flint scrapers, knives, arrowheads, borers, awls, and microliths. At the bottom of the pile was a stone hammer.

The hammer was constructed out of a long, heavy rectangular hard stone, bound to a stick by an ancient length of twine or cordage. The stone part of the hammer was stained a rusty colour. After laying out most of the stones and flints on top of the work bench Alistair decided to leave his discovery for now so that he could get on with the main task of opening the gate.

The padlock had a thick closed bar. He realised that sawing through it with a rusty hacksaw blade may take him some time. No time like the present, he thought and began cutting through the padlock. After what seemed an age, but in reality, was only five minutes, he stopped to rest. His arm muscles were getting sore. He examined the bar on the lock. He had managed to cut a groove about three millimetres deep. The lock bar itself was at least twenty millimetres thick. He was about to carry on when he heard something.

The wind was still strong and muffled his ears, but he thought he could hear a low and heavy breathing sound. Almost ape like. He turned around to look for any sign of where the breathing could be coming from. He guessed it was a trick of the wind as it blew through the bars of the gate. He carried on sawing into the lock. He stopped again, this time he heard a loud flapping sound. He turned and saw a large raven perched in a stately manner, on top of the snow dusted monolith. It seemed to be watching him with its shiny, obsidian eyes. He turned back to work on the lock.

The raven took off from its stony perch and landed on his shoulder where it began to attack him viciously. Dropping the hacksaw, Alistair used his hands and arms to bat the bird away. The creature flapped its ragged dark wings and soared aloft to land high up in the large ash tree but not before it had managed to draw blood from a small scalp wound where Alistair's hair had thinned out considerably during the last few years.

Still cursing at the raven, he dabbed at his scalp using a handkerchief from his pocket. Happy that no real harm had been done he retrieved the hacksaw that had come to rest between two of the railings of the gate. He noticed the saw blade had snapped from the impact of the drop. Cursing the raven again he went off to the workshop in search of a replacement saw blade but was unable to find one. He came out of the workshop carrying the stone hammer and held it up to threaten the raven. The raven had gone. He scanned the skies and the ash tree before placing the hammer on the ground next to the monolith.

******

Alistair had decided to go into town. At this time of year, the days were incredibly short and he needed to find a telephone so that he could report his power outage. He was hoping that the town itself had not been similarly affected by the recent winds otherwise he could be looking at a long spell without electricity. He also needed some more provisions, and maybe, if he was lucky, he might be able to purchase a better hacksaw.

The walk up the hill was difficult. The icy snow had created a slope that would be the dream of any tobogganing enthusiast. He had almost slipped over many times and the final few yards of dirt track merging with cobbled road he took very carefully.

Eventually, finding firm footing, Alistair proceeded to peruse the shops in the high street of Thornbarrow. Firstly, he entered the main grocery store where he purchased eggs, milk, bread, some sliced bacon and ham, and a variety of tinned essentials. His next stop was to a fishmonger where he purchased some kippers, he had it in mind to give the fish heads to the cat. His final call was to a hardware store run by the Agar brothers, according to the brightly painted signage.

The hardware store seemed packed with all the necessary tools and equipment that anyone should need. He waited patiently at the counter whilst a portly man wearing a teak coloured warehouse coat finished stacking tins of paint in the corner of the shop. Eventually the man finished his organisational chore and approached Alistair. "Good morning Sir, what you be after?"

"Good day. I am in need of a few bits and pieces. Do you have any candles?" asked Alistair.

"Candles, regular candles like?"

"Yes, just simple white candles, you see my electricity is out currently and until I am reconnected I will have to make do with candlelight." Alistair noticed that there were lights on inside the shop. "I see you are not similarly affected. Has most of the town avoided my misfortune?"

"No problems here, as far as I know Sir. Where about are you living, if I may ask?"

"I live down the hill, about three mile or so. The old Tudor house. You might know it." Alister stopped speaking and sneezed repeatedly. He took out a handkerchief and blew his nose.

"Aye, I know the place. You live in that house do you? You the one who recently bought it?" Alister finished wiping his nose before answering.

"Yes, I moved in this week. It's a great old place, but the weather!" Alister sneezed again.

"Looks like you caught a rook," said the storeman.

"I'm sorry. What do you mean?"

"You caught a rook. All that sneezing."

"Oh, sorry. I think I am coming down with a cold."

"Like I says, looks like you caught a rook." Alistair studied the middle-aged man before him. He had thin grey hair and a white moustache, neatly trimmed. He wore spectacles on a chain around his neck.

"Caught a rook. What an unusual saying."

"Just what we says around these parts. When somebody has a sniffle, we says they caught a rook!" Alistair remembered his encounter with the raven this very morning, his fingers found the sore wound made by the bird's beak. He rubbed his head lightly.

"Interesting. Oh, do you have a hacksaw by any chance?" The storeman scratched his head and walked over to some shelving at the back of the store muttering hacksaw over and over. He returned eventually carrying a shiny looking saw. He placed it on the counter.

"Will this be alright, only a gentleman came in yesterday and bought up all my other saws." Alistair handled the saw.

"Yes, this will do perfectly. So now it's just the candles if you have any." The storeman reached for a box below the counter muttering "candles, candles." He placed the box down in front of Alistair.

"How many candles you need Sir?"

"Good question. At this time, I have no idea how long I will be without power, so I suppose I will take quite a few. I think I will take the box if that's alright?"

"Fine by me Sir. Do you need a bag?" Alistair looked at his existing bag of provisions, it was quite full. He nodded and the storeman began to place the items into a large paper bag then rang up the tally on a cash register that sat perched on the end of the counter. Alistair paid for his goods and turned to leave the shop. "Fancy buying that old place," the storeman uttered. Alistair decided he would not question what he meant. He left the shop.

Ambling along the high street Alistair noticed the spire of the local church of St. Peter jutting upwards against the backdrop of rolling hills and trees. It wasn't all that far to reach and he decided to go and pay the church a visit before embarking on the treacherous descent back down to Olde Tudor.

There was a red telephone box outside the church. Alistair first made a call to the local electricity board and explained to them about his power outage. They informed him that they would look into it as soon as possible, and that he should call them again if he was still experiencing problems in the next day or so. He then made a second call to report his dead telephone line. He was given similar assurances to what the electrical board had said.

******

The churchyard looked splendid covered in a fine layer of snow. Winter could be one of the most beautiful times of the year thought Alistair as he walked down the path towards the church. He stopped to admire the soaring bell tower and noticed the adorning grotesque gargoyles as they peered down at him from their lofty perches. He decided he would like to look around inside the church, but first, he wanted to take a stroll through the churchyard.

Reading the old headstones was something that he had enjoyed doing ever since he was a small child. He thought, as he examined the old slate and stone gravestones, that it has always been a struggle facing up to the inevitable demise of the mortal body. Here amongst the buried was a good starting point if any to come to terms with one's own death he mused.

One tall and relatively recent headstone caught his eye. It was taller than many of the other headstones. He crossed over the snow-covered lawn to examine the epitaph. It read: *Lord Jesus. Of your charity pray for the soul of Reverend George Charles Redgrave Vicar of St. Peter for 27 years who died May 30 1939 aged 64 years.* This was surely the same reverend who had previously resided in Olde Tudor he thought. The same reverend who had written the journal that he had discovered in the wood shed.

His attention was then turned towards three smaller graves positioned to the right of the Reverend's gravestone. Each smaller grave had a flat tablet marker instead of an erect stone. He placed his bags down and crouched low so that he could brush away the fine snow with a gloved hand. The markings upon the three tablets were curious. There was no inscription. Each tablet had a number in Roman numerals, I, II, III. Underneath each number was simply the words: *PUT TO REST.*

The loud 'kaah-kaah' of a raven startled Alistair. He twisted around to catch sight of one of the large birds gliding to a perch on top of an old yew. The attack he had suffered this very morning had now made him wary of members of the Corvus family of birds. He stood up and made his way down the path towards the church.

The old, heavy oak door swung inwards. Alistair stepped inside the vestibule. The interior of the church was as he had hoped it would be. Above the main entrance on the inside of the vestibule was a statue of the virgin Mary. Directly opposite the entrance were a pair of large stone window frames filled with a beautiful stained glass depiction of Saint Peter with his hands clasped together, gazing upwards towards a shaft of heavenly golden light. The vaulted ceiling was adorned with carved wooden angelic figures, many with wings and trumpets.

As Alistair gazed upwards at the splendour of the church's ornamentation, a figure walked along the nave toward him. The man wore a tweed jacket, similar to Alistair's. He had dark yet greying hair at the temples, and he wore a clerical collar and carried a walking cane. Alistair smiled as the vicar approached him. "Good morning, I don't think I've had the pleasure," the vicar said as he greeted Alistair.

"Good morning, no, it's my first time here. Only recently moved into the locale," replied Alistair.

"Oh good, a new member of the congregation," the vicar said hopefully. "The Reverend John Mortimer," he said and reached out to shake Alistair's hand.

"Alistair Swift," he reciprocated, "moved into the old Tudor place, a mile or so down from the town."

"Yes, I know the place. It used to be the home of my predecessor, the Reverend George Redgrave, he was the vicar here for almost thirty years."

"Yes, I noticed the headstone in the church yard, twenty-seven years I think it said."

"Indeed. It was a shock to the locals when he. . . passed away. A terrible business. But tell me, what brings you to Thornbarrow?" Alistair placed both his heavy bags down onto a nearby pew,

"I have recently retired from my job teaching at a boy's school. I liked the look of the town, it's not too far from my only relative, my sister. Always fancied the country life."

"Well if you like rural, you couldn't have picked a better place. Other than the town itself, there's little more than agriculture, and the occasional wild wood or copse. And how is the old house? I believe it has stood empty for quite a while."

"Yes so I was told. It's a little cold and draughty. Everything I expected from a country house. But there are some curious oddities that came with it. In fact, it's what infused me to purchase the property."

"Ah! You must be talking about the standing stone?"

"Yes, quite an unusual thing to own I would say."

"Indeed it is. I do believe it to be the only remaining stone that used to form almost a complete Neolithic henge monument. The other stones were broken up at some time in the distant past and used as material to build many of the local cottages. In fact, a lot of the stone used to build this very church was once part of the circle I believe." Alistair was very much enthralled in what the vicar was telling him.

"That's really interesting. I didn't know that. There's also a cavern. Quite a ridiculous thing to find on one's own doorstep don't you think?"

"I did hear about that. The Reverend George Redgrave did some excavation of the cavern did he not? The locals say that it was once covered with earth creating a barrow. I dare say it's how the town got its name."

"Yes, I see what you mean," Alistair stopped briefly to blow his nose several times. "Excuse me, I seem to have caught a cold, not surprising in this weather! I would like to ask, did you know the previous vicar personally?"

"I met him of course after he had decided to retire. He remained at Saint Peter until I was ready to move into the new rectory. The Tudor property that you now own was his personal property. The original vicarage burnt to the ground before the war. We kept in touch from time to time. He was a great source of knowledge about the local families. I must say though, that shortly before his untimely death, he did seem a little troubled."

"Troubled? In what way?"

"Well, I went over to visit him on one occasion. He was feeling a bit under the weather. He had spent some considerable time investigating the cave you mentioned. I think he became a little obsessed with it. It was one of those obsessions that takes over a man's life. The poor chap would go without food and turn away visitors, even from his own family because he was so eager to complete his excavation of the site."

"I found his notebook. I have started reading it. I must say it is a very thorough piece of work. He would have made quite an archaeologist if he hadn't had the calling."

"Yes, he was always interested in the local history, and especially of the church itself." The Reverend Mortimer motioned for Alistair to follow him towards the church exit. "There is something I'd like to show you, if you have the time." Alistair collected up his bags,

"Of course, what is it?" he asked intrigued.

"Well George apparently excavated three graves inside the cavern. He told me that he intended to bury the remains in this churchyard."

Alistair found himself standing before the three, curious stone tablet grave markers again. The Reverend Mortimer used his walking cane to point them out to Alistair. "He placed the markers for the graves here. This patch was his own plot. I remember it well. He came to me one spring morning, he was shaking, and obviously unwell with a fever. He asked if I would help him to set out the stone markers. He brought them with him, he had carried them one at a time all the way from his house! We set out the slabs as you see them today. A week later I paid him a visit as I was worried about him. Whilst I was with him he brought out three boxes from his tool shed. He showed them to me. Inside one of them was a lot of old bones, including the remains of three skulls. At some point, he had labelled each and every bone carefully.

"These were bones he had found inside the cavern?" asked Alistair.

"Yes, that's what he said. He was adamant that they required a burial within hallowed ground. He practically begged me to help him. I realised the poor chap was not himself so I naturally agreed.

"Why do you suppose he wanted them buried here?"

"I have absolutely no idea. The poor chap was so anxious. He tipped the contents of the box out onto his parlour floor. He then asked me for my help in sorting the bones into three distinct piles. I remember him spending a considerable amount of time ensuring that all the bones were in the correct order and heap. He did this with extraordinary diligence. Each heap was then placed into its own box and sealed. We then discussed a suitable scriptural reading that he asked me to deliver after the burial. He wanted to return to Saint Peter immediately to bury the boxes. I told him that I did not think he was in any fit state to do such a thing. I advised him to take to his bed and wait until his fever had broken. I offered to take the boxes back to the church and store them for him until he felt better. After some persuasion he agreed."

"So, the bones, they were buried here?" said Alistair pointing at the three graves.

"I'm afraid not, you see I stored the boxes inside a large chest at the back of the nave. I thought they would be safe enough in there until George was fit. The Saturday following my visit to George I was preparing a sermon and took a walk around

Saint. Peter as I usually do. I then noticed the chest in the nave where I had put the bones. The lid was ripped off with such ferocity it left splinters of wood littering the floor in all directions."

"Good lord. What had happened?"

"The boxes were missing. I don't know why, but when I saw the mess of that chest I had an uneasy feeling and I decided to pay George a visit. When I got to his house, your house now. I found him lying in the garden. Close to that monolith. It looked as though he had been attacked. The poor chap had been beaten to death. Local policeman suspected a robbery. But as he lived alone there was no way of knowing if anything had been taken." The reverend Mortimer began to feel a little guilty at painting such a bleak picture about the demise of the previous resident of Alistair's new home. Alistair assured him that he was fine with the details and that he wasn't superstitious. He had no qualms about living in a house that had such a gloomy history.

Alistair and the reverend Mortimer talked some more before Alistair said that it was high time he was heading back home. It was almost midday and he was eager to try out the new hacksaw blade on the padlocked gate before sundown. He had mentioned to Mortimer the unfortunate business of his power outage and telephone problem. The Reverend kindly said that he would make a call on Alistair's behalf to the electrical board to save him a walk back into town.

4

Alistair had been busy since returning to Olde Tudor. First, he had unpacked the provisions he had acquired from his morning in the town. Next, he had lit a fire to warm the house. Smokey had curled up to sleep in front of it after greedily lapping up a saucer of milk and chewing on the head of a kipper. Happy that the fire was adequately stocked with fuel enough to last an hour at least, he lit some candles to illuminate the house. He then took the hacksaw and went outside to continue working on the cavern gate.

His arm was aching as he rhythmically sliced through the padlock. He stopped to wipe sweat from his brow with a pocket handkerchief then realised that he was not perspiring due to the exercise. He had a temperature. In fact, he was beginning to feel quite shabby as his fever was getting the better of him. Nevertheless, he aimed to finish the task before him.

A loud *CLACK* signified that he had managed to finally sever the shackle. He twisted the body of the padlock and unhooked the remains of the shackle from the gate. With his free hand, he pushed the gate. A loud squeal issued from its oxidised hinges as it swung inwards towards the dark interior of the cave.

Back at the house Alistair tried to light the hurricane lamp. The previous time he had used the lamp he had managed to wind the wick too low whilst extinguishing the flame. He would have to take the lamp to pieces in order to reattach the wick onto the toothed cog. This operation would take time. The light outside was already beginning to falter. He decided to fit some of the candles he had bought from the hardware shop into an elaborate steel candelabra that had been left at the house. Taking the candelabra, and the matches he made his way back to the cave.

He had only covered the first few yards of the cave when he began to see the paintings. Holding the lighted candelabra up against the cave wall he studied the pictures. They were exactly as described in Redgrave's notebook. The colours were so vibrant and fresh. He could hardly believe that they were in fact over seventeen thousand years old. A wind eased itself along the passage where Alistair stood bathed in the incandescent glow from the candles. The wind's playful fingers tampered with the candles. Fearing that they would be extinguished he lowered them protectively before moving on.

A little further along, the stone passage opened out into a moderately sized chamber, about as large as a two-storey house. He gazed upwards. The ceiling of the chamber was adorned with calcium carbonate formations produced through slow precipitation. Stalactites, stalagmites, and an array of soda straws were a delight to his exploring eyes. The flickering candlelight created surreal long shadows on the rocky floor. The walls gave off a weak phosphorescence as Alistair passed by with the candelabra.

The candlelight picked out more wall paintings towards the back of the chamber. As he moved across, carefully trying to avoid tripping on the stalagmites that covered the floor, he then noticed the piles of rocks. There were three piles in total. He examined the rock piles. Each pile appeared to be constructed from four large flat rocks laid together in a slanted position that formed a triangular structure. Smaller loose stones and rocks had then been piled on top and around both ends. He then saw the remains of three cardboard boxes. They had been ripped open. Curious as to what might be underneath the rocks, he began to remove some stones at one end of one of the rock piles.

Crouching low, he removed a candle from the candelabra and held it inside the gap he had created. He jumped with fright as the light picked out a sepulchral bony face, its dark eye sockets animated by the candlelight. For a moment, he experienced trembling and his heart was thumping, calming himself he reached into the stones and removed the small skull.

Calmer now, he turned the skull in his hands to examine it. It was small enough to be a child's he thought. The skull contained a label. The label read *B-2*. He moved over to the two other stone piles. A brief excavation revealed two further skeletal subjects. Only one of the other skulls was intact. One was badly broken and only the front part remained containing the frontal head plate and the facial maxilla complete with the nasal cavity. The lower jaw was missing. Again, the bones had labels attached.

Above the rock piles were the paintings he had first noticed. They depicted stick-like drawings of people. They appeared to be dancing around a large towering object. He wondered if this was a representation of the single stone monolith outside. There were many paintings of what appeared to be people lying on the ground. For some reason, he assumed the picture to be telling a story about sacrifice as the figures on the ground appeared to be partly dismembered.

Underneath the figures were a set of hand stencils. There were three pairs of hands in total. One large pair, then a slender smaller pair, and finally a child sized set. Each set of hands were positioned directly above one of the rock piles. Alistair realised that the hand stencils were from a family, and the family had been buried within this chamber. He was looking at their graves.

He reached up and placed his own hand against the larger of the hand stencils. His own hand fell short slightly against the ghostly negative shape. He then became aware of a sound. It was the sound of rapid heavy breathing. Low guttural breaths. He snatched his hand away from the cold rock wall. The sound came again. He held out the candelabra before him to scan the chamber. The shadows played tricks with his mind making him think that he could sense movement amongst the stalagmites and stalactites as they cast oddly distorted shadows across the walls and the floor.

His eyes widened and his eyebrows shot upwards. He jumped back from the rock piles. The breathing came again and now it seemed to be all around him. He searched for an animal of some kind. It had to be an animal he kept on telling himself (what else could explain the shredded boxes?). The subterranean wind channelled from outside snuffed out two of the three candles. Immediately he cupped his hand around the one surviving flame to protect it. He fumbled for his box of matches in his jacket pocket. He heard them drop to the floor. He realised that if he moved his hand to try and retrieve the matches, the candle flame would be extinguished plunging him into total darkness, and alone, with the breathing.

Racing along the passage, his heart pounding, his lungs gasping and gulping for air, he detached the lighted candle and dropped the candelabra discarding it underfoot as he lurched onwards towards the exit. The wind outside continued to play with the rusty gate, the creaking hinges were somewhat of a comfort to Alistair, blocking out the sound of the heavy breathing that seemed to follow him all along the passage.

He shot out from the entrance to the cavern dropping the candle and clutching his chest. Quickly he fastened the gate then backed away from it hungrily gulping at the frosty evening air. He kept his eyes on the cave as he walked backwards towards the house. He was half expecting to see some nightmarish creature slither out from the cave. His imagination was working time and a half.

Now almost calm once more he continued to catch his breath. He leaned against the white plank door to the house as fat flat flakes of snow began to fall. The wind was whipping up again. The gate continued to rattle. Smokey, his adopted cat came to greet him at the door. Rubbing his body against him. He went inside.

After eating his supper, Alistair reloaded the fire with logs and set about building a second fire in the bedroom. He was now beginning to feel more unwell by the hour. His head was starting to ache badly, and his throat had become almost too painful to swallow. He made himself a pot of tea on the stove and settled down by the fireside with Smokey on his lap.

Whilst sipping his tea to ease his sore throat he thought about the cave, the stone graves, and the breathing sound. He had convinced himself that the noises were created by a subterranean wind effect. It was best that he kept this thought as any fanciful thinking would prevent him from ever going near the cave again. And he had to. His curiosity was sparked.

It was almost eleven o'clock. Alistair took his empty teapot and cup out into the kitchen. He glanced out of the window near the sink. The snow was settling thick. In only three hours it had fell to the depth of what he thought looked like three to four inches and there was no sign of it stopping anytime soon. He checked his phone line again. Dead. He decided to retire to his bed, his aching body needed rest. He was shivering. Carrying some logs with him he climbed the stairs to the bedroom.

He lay reading the journal of the reverend George Redgrave some more as the fire crackled noisily in the grate. The final pages were filled with prayers, and incoherent ramblings. One passage caught his eye - *Ever since I found them, moved them. I don't feel as though I've ever been alone* – he skipped a few incomprehensible sentences and then read – *What does it want? I ask over and over to leave me be. Oh Lord what does it want?*

A large spark burst from a log in the fire grate causing his heart to skip a beat. Rubbing his head, he closed the journal and snuffed out a bedside candle using his fingertips. He drew the bedcovers up to his chin then settled down to catch some sleep. A good night's sleep ought to make him feel better he thought.

Alistair didn't get a good rest. His fever produced a fragmented night's sleep. A sleep made up of disjointed nightmares. Some of them vivid and frightening. In one dream, he was standing in the centre of Sheffield. The air raid sirens were still wailing their frightening tones, *mmMMMMMOOOOOOOOOoooooooOOOOOOOOOOO OWWWWWWWWWWWWWWWWA AAAAAAAAAAAAAAAAAH.*

The building in front of him had just been hit. It was now reduced to rubble and flames. He watched as survivors, covered in ash and pulverised concrete dust, and many of them wearing ripped and ragged clothing, staggered around the debris. Alistair suddenly realised that the devastation before him used to be the home of his fiancée, his one and only true love.

Instinctively he ran and climbed on top of the rubble. With his bare hands, he heaved and cast great chunks of concrete from the top of the pile searching for her, praying to God that she had survived.

A woman staggered passed him, she was almost naked and covered in dust mixed with blood. He grabbed her and turned her so he could see her face. It wasn't Evelyn. The woman wobbled once Alistair had released her. She steadied herself by placing a bloodied hand against the only part of a fragmented wall that was still standing. She left a print of her own hand, like a red marker of death.

He continued to dig for Evelyn shouting her name. When he had removed some of the larger concrete and brick slabs he saw a fragment of bright blue material poking through the layered pulverised bricks. Evelyn's dress was blue. He clawed and scraped back the bricks. The last few, once removed revealed the body beneath. It might have been Evelyn, but he had no way of knowing. Her face was a skull with dust-grey matted hair. She still wore a hair clip. He backed away from her horrified. She started to move, to sit upright. Her one remaining arm reached out for him. It gripped his ankle tightly. Each tapered bony finger wore a label.

Alistair woke from his dream screaming. He was covered in fever sweat. He opened his eyes. His room was dark. The fire in the grate had reduced to a few glowing embers. He reached over for a glass of water and took a sip. He winced and clenched his teeth. His sore throat felt raw. He pushed back the blanket and lay back on his pillow. He could feel fresh ripples of sleep forming as his consciousness ebbed away.

In a new dream, he found himself tethered on top of what felt like a flat rock. He was naked and was outside. He was cold. So cold. He craned his neck to see what he could. He saw that he was surrounded by a henge of standing stones. A short, stocky man wearing animal skins was standing beside him. He had a bag of sorts made from skins. The man was handing out flat flint stones to a crowd of similarly dressed men, women and children who were all making their way to the centre of the henge.

The man with the flint bag then held his hands up to the sky. He shouts something incomprehensible. The rest of the crowd look upwards. Alistair looked up. He saw the moon. It is tinged with a red glow.

The crowd all start chanting as euphoria appears to spread from one to the other. Then they turn on Alistair. One by one each of them begin to use their flint tool on Alistair's body. He screamed as he was slowly skinned alive.

******

The next morning Alistair woke feeling worse with his illness. The headaches were more intense. His nose was blocked and his sinuses were heavily congested exacerbating his headaches. The random cycles of sweats then chills were uncomfortable enough, and his muscles ached. Wrapping a woollen bedsheet around himself, and sliding his feet into a pair of slippers, he slowly made his way down to the kitchen.

He intended to make himself a pot of tea as his throat was still painful and very dry. But mostly because the house was freezing cold. Ice clung to the inside of every window. The coldness from the stone flagged floor was already beginning to penetrate upwards through his slippers.

He clumsily cleaned out the wood stove and added fresh kindling. Next, he looked for his box of matches. After a fruitless search, he remembered that he had dropped them in the cave during the previous day's exploration. Realising he was unable to light the stove, or in fact anything in the house, he slammed down his tea caddy in frustration.

Parting the kitchen curtains, he peered outside through the iced leaded window panes. The snow was deep. Almost a couple of feet in places. The wind had caused drifting. He opened the back door and a pile of snow toppled inwards covering his feet. Shaking the snow off his slippers he closed the door. Smokey entered the kitchen, his meows and purrs signified that he was hungry again.

Feeling disheartened after imagining what a nice treat a pot of hot tea and a fried kipper would have been, Alistair went over to the small pantry to collect a bottle of milk. He poured some into a saucer on the kitchen floor. Smokey lapped it up greedily.

Still wrapped in his bedclothes Alistair searched high and low for a second box of matches. He poked about in the dead fire grates for a trace of a glowing cinder. He thought if he found one he might be able to use it to coax the woodstove into life. There was none. What was he supposed to do now he pondered? Rub sticks together like a caveman?

He tried his phone line again but it was still dead, as were the lights and other electrics in the house. The wind had picked up again, it was whipping around the house cooling it down even further. He thought that the best course of action was to go back to his bed, and keep as warm as he could. He was feeling terrible. He desperately hoped that his power and communication lines would soon be remedied, but the weather outside probably meant more delays.

He weakly carried a ceramic jug over to the sink, he intended to fill it with water so that he could place it by his bedside. Always best to keep your fluids up, he remembered his doctor once telling him. He turned the tap but nothing came out. The pipes must be frozen. He returned to the pantry and took the only remaining milk and some sliced ham. He returned to his bed. After eating a couple of slices of ham, he settled back into his bed and fell into a spate of broken sleep.

He woke with a hacking cough. Each cough made his head throb. The light was failing in the bedroom. He picked up his wristwatch from the bedside cabinet. He could barely make out that it read 3:30. He had slept most of the day. He Took hold of the half bottle of milk and took small sips, small enough that his aching throat would allow. He used his only remaining handkerchief to clear his nose.

Glancing at the dead fire grate, he realised that he had to go back into the cave to find the matches. His illness was steadily getting worse. He might catch his death he thought If he didn't get himself warm. And he would have to do it whilst he still had the strength. But not tonight. The weather was frightful. And the night had almost fallen. He would try in the morning. As he thought about this course of action he became aware of a sound.

Lying with the bedclothes pulled tightly around his head, partly to keep himself warm, but mostly to obscure the ghastly sounds that had begun to fill his bedroom. Alistair lay paralysed with fear. The breathing had started suddenly. The same bestial snorts and pants that had frightened him whilst he was in the cave. They sounded as though they were just outside of his bedroom window. The ancient ash, all old and gnarled was the only thing that could provide height for any creature outside that wanted to taunt him. And taunt him it did.

He didn't dare look across to the window. With only the ghost of the day's light lingering he feared that if he did look he might see it. The thing that his subconscious mind had concocted back in the cave. The thing that he had been trying so desperately hard to push back further and further into the dark crepuscular recesses of his mind, but was failing with every new second to do so. "Away!" he croaked hoarsely, "for pity's sake, leave me be!"

With his final words, the breathing stopped. With his heart in his mouth, he lowered the bedsheet just enough for him to take a gulp of cool air. If he had light in his room he would have seen his exhaled breath hang before him, a frozen nebulous cloud of vapour, slowly dissipating away like a phantom searching for a dark place in which to hide itself.

As he sat up in bed, still breathing hard, palpitations thumping against his festering chest cavity a new sound rang out. The sound was outside. Some distance from the house. He knew exactly the source and cause of the sound. It was the gate to the cavern slamming shut.

******

It took Alistair some time to drag his shivering body out of bed. It was six in the morning. Like the previous day, he wrapped the woollen bed sheet around him and donned his slippers. He stood up slowly, then coughed up a sickening globule of sticky mucous. He saw it land on the floor beside his bed. He felt disgusted by his own malaise.

The first thing he did was try the light switches to the bedroom. Still no power. He moved over to the window, he thought about checking the situation with the snow. Suddenly he remembered the fear he had gone through during the night. The laboured breathing outside. He withdrew his fingers from the curtains. He had no intention of looking at that ash tree just yet.

Smokey was purring frantically at the sight of Alistair. There was a yellow puddle on the floor in the kitchen. Alistair realised that the poor animal had been shut in for the best part of a day whilst he was in bed. The cat hadn't eaten either. "You poor thing," he said in between bouts of coughing. "Let me fix you something to eat and drink." He sacrificed the final kipper knowing he could not cook it and eat it himself. There was no milk left. He tried the tap at the sink. It was still frozen. Then he had an idea.

Opening the back door, he packed some snow into a jug then set it down by the sink. He thirstily ate some snow himself, the cooling effect of the snow eased his throat slightly. He looked at the jug of snow. He realised it could take some time to thaw into water that he could use for himself or Smokey. He then opened the back door to let the cat out. Smokey left the house hesitantly due to the deep crisp snow outside. Closing the door Alistair shivered then coughed some more. He then went to get dressed. Wearing his warmest clothing, and wrapped in a blanket he ventured outside.

The whiteness of the snow was blinding. He walked through the garden and all the way over to the cave. The snow had formed sporadic drifts in the most inappropriate places. One had blocked access to the workshop door. Another had half climbed to the top of the monolith. Alistair slowly approached the cave.

The gate was shut and he was horrified to see a trail leading out from the cave and continuing to the house. The track consisted of deep pits. Not an animal's he thought. They were set out in a human like gait. The sight of those tracks validated his experiences. Something was in the cave. It had crawled, no. Walked out. It had walked in bold strides towards his house. He surmised that it had climbed the ash tree where its haunting breathing had plagued him.

With his eyes, he followed the trail past the gate and into the cave. He hated the idea of venturing back into that bleak grotto. He did need those matches. He opened the gate. Smokey joined him at the mouth of the cave. He was glad of the company.

The first few steps were not so bad as the growing daylight filtered through illuminating his course. Smokey ran on ahead. He tried to call to him but his voice fuelled more coughing that stopped him in his tracks and doubled him up. His chest was feeling very sore and the deep coughing had caused his back and sides to ache.

Once the fit was over he straightened and carried on.

He had to use his hands to feel the rest of the way. He tripped on many stalagmites and concluded that he must be in the main chamber. If he remembered correctly, the rock graves were directly in front of him just forward of the back wall of the cavern. His feet eventually found them. He got to his hands and knees and searched about the floor.

He couldn't see anything but solid blackness. He imagined that he could actually feel the darkness with his fingertips. His left hand sensed something. It felt like cardboard. Delighted he snatched up the object then discarded it when he realised what it was. It was a piece of one of those old shredded cardboard boxes. One that was used to house Redgrave's collection of labelled bones. He continued to search frantically. He didn't want to be in this cold dark place any longer than he had to be. And then it happened. The thing he had been dreading the most.

He tried to run but tripped on a stalagmite. He stood up again, although he couldn't see it, he knew his hand had been injured. The breathing seemed to be coming from all around him. He had no strength to run. The best he could muster was a feeble jog as he felt the walls with his trembling hands like a blind man feels his way around an unfamiliar place. His blanket snagged on a stalagmite, stealing it away from his shoulders. He kept on following the rock wall, he knew eventually he would turn the corner and then he would see the light.

The morning light spilled down the last few yards of the passage. Alistair continued his trot, dragging his leg from fever induced fatigue. His breath was visible to him as he passed through it in his last desperate attempt to get out the cave.

He leaned on the gate whilst he caught his breath. Even the fear of whatever horror was lurking in the hole behind him was not enough to give him the power to move right now. He stood erect when he heard the shrill cry of a wounded animal. "Smokey!" he called into the gaping maw. He cupped his hands around his lips, "Smokey, Smoke . . ." his cries turned to coughs. He knew if that was Smokey crying out, then what had happened to him, in the cave, had sounded bad, final. He knew Smokey wasn't coming back.

Perched atop a stool in the kitchen, Alistair felt disparaged. Not only had he lost his blanket and hadn't been able to locate the matches, he had lost his only form of companionship. Determined to help himself, he decided to try to get back up to town. If he had the strength to do this, then he might be able to find a doctor who could prescribe him something to help with his malady.

Back outside, Alistair had used a fallen branch from the Ash tree as a walking stick. It gave him something to lean on at least. He slowly trudged through the deep snow. The shoes he wore were hardly suitable for the weather, they provided little insulation from the snow. He reached the garden gate and pushed it open. Stepping carefully onto the snow-covered verge he scanned the road that climbed up to the town.

The town was out of sight but he knew it was about a mile or so upwards. The road and surrounding fields were covered by an undisturbed dazzling coat of snow that he thought resembled whipped cream. He chuckled to himself at the thought but stopped laughing when his brief jollity turned to more fits of hacking coughing. Once he had re-composed himself, he made his first tentative steps onto the slippery road.

The lane was icy, and covered with snow. His feet were slipping with each and every footfall. His shoes had hardly any grip and his toes were already numbing. After a few steps, he heard a flapping sound. He glanced upwards to see the familiar plumage of a large black bird perch on a nearby sycamore. The snow fell from the branches as the creature hopped sideways. He wondered if it was the same bird that had once attacked him in the garden. Keeping one eye on the raven he used his stick for support as he continued his ascent.

The first time he fell he hit the ground hard, landing on his right hip. He slid down almost to the gate of his garden. Slowly he stood and brushed away the snow from his coat. "Damned infernal season!" he cursed. More determined than ever he started again.

This time each step produced pain in his hip. His body was already aching from his sickness. Every rib, intercostal muscle, bone, and joint hurt. Every breath threatened another round of painful coughing. The branch, not being a correct walking stick, also began to slip and slide whenever he placed his weight on it. He fell again, landing on the same bruised hip bone. This time he let out a cry of pain.

He sat in the snow and rubbed at his hip and leg. It was so quiet in the lane. As he sat there he wondered why it always seemed quiet after a heavy snowfall. Generally, there are not all that many winter people outside, they were probably all sitting beside fires all warm and snug inside their homes. He thought about one of his colleagues at the school, Peter Davenport. Davenport taught science. They had once had a conversation regarding the peacefulness following a wintery covering at the school. Davenport had theorised that the quietness was caused by the ability of the snow to absorb soundwaves. He had said something about snowflakes stacking up, leaving lots of air spaces between. It seemed a good enough answer he thought as he once again heaved himself to his feet.

Realising that he wasn't making much progress and also noticing the weak winter sun sitting low in the sky, he thought he'd best get going again as soon, dusk would fall. He didn't want to face another dark bitterly cold night.

As he made his way slowly up the lane, he noticed the raven had begun following him, flying from tree to tree, hopping from branch to branch. The action of the bird perturbed him. He found himself no longer concentrating on keeping his balance on the ice beneath his feet. Instead, he was keeping a close eye on the raven.

The raven's first dive took him by complete surprise. The bird swooped down and clawed at his shoulder with its talons before soaring aloft and perching safely on a high branch of another sycamore. Alistair managed to keep upright this time. But only just. He carried on trudging up the slope. He glanced back and could still see Olde Tudor. He had barely made any progress. He tried to quicken his step but this caused him to cough. To prevent too much pain from his aching sides he bent low whilst he coughed. He didn't see the raven before it attacked again.

This time the bird struck the side of Alistair's cheek. It drew a sharp scratch. Alistair stopped coughing and wiped at his face. His fingers were wet with his own blood. He turned and saw the raven returning to its temporary roost, springing along a high branch. The bird seemed almost in joy. Its harsh, grating, cawing was not unlike a mirthful cackle.

Alistair gripped his stick in preparation for the next attack. It came quickly. He watched as the bird swooped low, its long pointed black beak thrust forwards like a jousting pole. As the raven came close Alistair stepped to the side, and used the stick as a weapon attempting to strike the raven. He missed the bird completely.

The raven altered the course of its flight and soared upwards, then it came for him again. Alistair held the stick out front. Before he could wield the weapon, his feet slipped from under him. Landing on his buttocks heavily, he dropped the stick as he slid all the way down the lane only coming to rest at his own garden wall.

Alistair slowly got to his feet using the wall as support. He was cold, wet, and shivering and feeling extremely disheartened. He had failed to make it to town. He was injured. Still sick, he faced another dark and miserable night at the house. Just to destroy any thoughts of a further attempt to get to town, the raven swooped past him and landed on the old ash tree in his garden. Even if he had managed to strike the bird with his stick giving it a terminal injury, he felt that his energy resources were now reaching a critical state. He barely had enough strength to walk from the wall to the house, but he found it somehow.

In the pantry were a few tins that contained soup, beans, and fruit. He picked up the tin of beans, and took a fork, and a tin opener out of a cutlery drawer. He sat his weak frame down on a chair next to a dead fire grate. He struggled to open the tin, his wrist was aching as were all his joints. After a few attempts, he finally managed to remove most of the lid.

He ate some of the beans straight from the tin using a fork. His illness had numbed his taste buds. He ate half of the cold meal before another round of coughing forced him to stop. He stared longingly at the ashes in the fire grate. He wished that he could stretch out his hand and feel the warmth from a cheerful fire. Then he had an idea.

It seemed preposterous to Alistair, that he had not thought of it sooner. Wrapping himself in as many warm clothes as he could find he left the house and stepped once more into the cold effulgent brightness outside. He made his way over to the workshop. Once he reached the workshop he used his right leg to kick away the snow drift that was hugging the door and wall. He then unlocked the door using the key, and never for a moment taking his eyes away from the raven that was still perched in the ash tree.

Once inside the workshop he closed the door. It was gloomy inside. The night was sliding in fast. He made his way over to the workbench, the flint tools were still arranged as he had left them. He gathered a few and placed them back into the box lined with straw before leaving the workshop.

He stuffed the pockets of his coat with kindling wood and a few larger pieces. He still had enough wood back at the house. He was going to use the flint pieces to try to light a fire. As he turned to leave the wood store he heard the crash of a gate. The noise almost made him drop the box of flints he was carrying.

He studied the gate to the cave, it was closed. But the noise had indicated that something had opened it and closed it noisily. Maybe it was the wind, he thought trying to deceive himself. He began to trudge back through the deep snow to the house. When he got to the door he stopped. It was slightly ajar. He was sure he had closed it behind him. He studied the snow on the ground. There were a few tracks all mingled together. It was difficult to say if there were any prints other than his own. Tentatively, he stepped inside the house and closed the door.

5

Alistair tipped all the dry straw from the box into the fire grate. He arranged the straw into the shape of a bird's nest inside the grate. He had built similar fires whilst teaching at the boy's school during camping excursions. He then fetched a sharp knife from the kitchen and began to scrape the knife along one edge of a flint tool he had selected. The scraping had produced a small pile of flint shavings that he kept towards the middle of the straw nest. Turning the flint over he began to scrape down the other side using the knife producing sparks. The sparks began to hit the shavings and suddenly the straw caught fire.

Quickly and carefully, he began to place the smallest pieces of kindling wood onto the burning straw. As the small twigs caught fire, he added slightly larger sticks and continued to build the fire until the whole grate was ablaze. Happy with his handiwork he knelt to feel the warmth on his face. The first warmth he had felt in days.

He lit many candles before taking one of them into the kitchen. He used the candle to start a fire in the wood stove. Once the stove was hot he took a saucepan and into it he emptied the remaining beans from the tin he had eaten from earlier. Then he filled a kettle from the jug that contained the snow melt and put some tea leaves in a pot. His mood began to perk up. He was feeling warm, and soon he would have some hot food. He almost drooled at the prospect, even though his meal would only comprise of two thirds a can of baked beans.

He sat next to the fire for a good hour following his supper and pot of tea. His face glowed from the heat the burning wood threw out at him. Even though the feeling was almost uncomfortable, he remained where he sat, soaking up the warmth.

Outside he could hear the wind beginning to whip up again. There was also the sound of tiny crystals of ice pattering against the curtain covered windows. It had started to snow again. Another sound however, made his blood run into icy creeps. From somewhere, and he was unable to discern exactly the whereabouts, he could hear that odious breathing again. Only this time the snorts and gasps didn't emanate from outside. They came from inside the house.

Weakly, he rose from his seat and scanned the room. There was nothing to be seen. His heart began to race. He remembered the door being slightly ajar on his return from the woodstore. Now he was faced with the real prospect that the horror from the cave, whatever it might be, could be inside the house with him.

He grabbed the poker from out of the fire. The pointed hammered end was glowing a vermillion orange. He picked up a lighted candle stick and slowly searched around the house. The kitchen was quiet, other than the crackling burning wood from within the stove. He made his way to the bottom of the stairs. "Hello. . ." he called before some violent coughing almost made him drop the candlestick. Recomposed, he called out again. This time he heard a muffled dragging sound from above his head. The poker was still hot and he bravely climbed the wooden steps to the landing.

The bathroom's peace was only disturbed by a dripping tap. He screwed the tap shut tight. The dripping ceased. Holding the candle in a shaky hand he made his way over to the master bedroom. Inside he was faced with a gut-wrenching sight. Smokey, his adopted feline companion was laid out at the end of his bed. He had been meticulously skinned, and fortunately, was quite dead. He wretched at the gory sight.

Before Alistair could react further to the display in his room the breathing came again. He turned to see a shadow out on the landing. It appeared to be cast from something descending the wooden stairs. But there was no sound of footfalls on the steps. Too scared to move he just stood watching until the last trace of a shadow had disappeared.

Still rooted to the spot he heard the sound of the back-door open but not close. He raced over to the bedroom window and parted the curtains. It was so dark outside he could only see his own terrified reflection on each of the leaded panes, illuminated by the candle he carried. He left the bedroom and went downstairs.

The door was blowing on its hinges, snow was drifting in and settling on the kitchen floor. For a moment, in his fear and his sickness he just stood and watched as the wind played with the door. Awakening from his catatonic state he pushed the door shut and slid the bolt across just in time to hear the clash of the cavern gate outside. It had returned home, he thought. Whatever had been in his house had gone back to the cave. The uninvited was gone. For now.

A fire now blazed in the grate of his bedroom. The room itself was illuminated by many candles. Smokey had been wrapped up in a blanket and placed onto the windowsill. He decided that he would take him to the woodstore in the morning and leave him there. Eventually he would dig him a grave, when he had sufficiently recovered from his illness. He went down into the kitchen to fetch a glass of water.

In only a few seconds, he was reduced to that of a cowering and pathetic figure. Through a gap in the curtain he saw a shape pass by the window. The crunching of feet through crystalized snow outside caused him to tremble with fear. And then there came a rapping on the door. Alistair ran over to the door to check the bolt was still fastened and secure. He was shaking uncontrollably, he pressed his back against the door and began to cough. "Go away, leave me in peace! For pity's sake, leave me alone!" he cried. The rapping continued. He could now hear a voice accompanying the rapping from beyond the door. The voice was calling to him.

He listened to the voice. It was calling to him by his full name. "Mister Swift, Mister Swift. This is Reverend Mortimer. Are you alright? Mister Swift?" Alistair stood and listened to the voice. His mind was fuzzy due to his illness, but the name,

Mortimer. He remembered. The Vicar at St. Peter. He turned and reached for the bolt but then froze. Why would Mortimer be here, at his house? His fingertips left the cold bolt and returned to his side. It must be a trick, he thought. That horror, from the cavern, it was trying to trick him. It wanted to get inside.

The rapping continued, but this time on the window above the kitchen sink. He turned and saw a shadow was peering in at the window, through the parted curtain. "I can see you, please, open the door!" the voice rang out. Alistair bravely walked to the window. The face that was pressed up against the old diamond panes was that of the Reverend Mortimer. Alistair reached out towards the window,

"Is . . . is it you? Really? Is it you?" he asked meekly.

"My god! You look terrible. Open the door and let me in," the face shouted then disappeared from the window. The rapping continued at the door. This time Alistair slowly drew back the bolt and pulled open the door.

The Reverend Mortimer hurriedly entered the house. Alistair slammed shut the door and frantically secured it using the bolts. He was breathing heavily as he finished. He turned to see the Reverend removing his coat and hat, both of which were sprinkled with fine snow.

Placing his coat and hat down on top of the dining table, the Reverend leaned his cane against one of the chairs before approaching Alistair. "I can't decide if you look sick, or terrified, or both!"

he said with concern in his tone. "I was worried you might be struggling without power in this weather. When I saw that my thermometer in the garden was reading minus five." Alistair just sat himself down on a chair by the dining table. "You don't look at all well my friend. How long have you been like this?" asked the Reverend. Alistair coughed then clutched at his chest as if in pain.

"Days. Since I was at the church," he answered and continued to cough. Mortimer picked up his own coat and placed it around Alistair's shoulders.

"Come, let's get you sat by the fire, I take it you have lit a fire?" Alistair just pointed at the doorway that lead to the parlour. Mortimer helped Alistair to his feet and walked him through into the parlour so that he could sit himself down. The fire was burning low and Mortimer threw some more wood into the grate. He noticed that the wood basket was almost empty. "I shall go and fetch you some more wood. I remember the old wood shed from the days I used to visit with George. Shan't be long." Mortimer picked up the wood basket, Alistair gripped him weakly by his arm,

"Be . . . careful," he said.

"Of course," came Mortimer's reply. He studied Alistair for a moment, Alistair released his grip. Mortimer remembered when he had seen such pain in a man's face before. For a moment, he thought he was looking into the face of the late Reverend George Redgrave.

Alistair rose from his seat and followed Mortimer as he left the house via the back door. Mortimer had left the door slightly open so that he could simply re-enter once he had fetched more wood. The door was bumping against the latch in the wind. Alistair desperately wanted to close it. He was afraid that whatever abhorrence that had entered his house before the arrival of Mortimer, could do so again. He waited a while. Give Mortimer a chance he thought. He should be back in a minute. The door continued to bump against the latch.

After waiting a full five minutes, he went over and pushed the door shut. As he did so he became aware of the sound of feet stomping through the thick snow outside. The footfalls were approaching the door. He hoped that it was Mortimer and that he had returned unscathed. The handle of the door jerked up and down. Then there came a pounding on the door. Alistair froze for a moment. He waited for the familiar voice of Mortimer before he opened the door.

Mortimer had returned with a basket full of wood and set it down next to the fire. He was concerned about Alistair's condition. He had made up a pot of coffee and set it to rest on the stove in the kitchen, but then he decided that Alistair could do with something stronger. Alister told him that there was a bottle of brandy in the pantry.

Mortimer fetched two glasses and poured himself and Alistair a large glassful. "I shall stay here tonight. I am concerned that you do not look at all well. I will make sure you are alright and I shall return to town in the morning to fetch a doctor. I have my car outside." Alistair drank his brandy in one large gulp. "Steady on old chap," said Mortimer, and he refilled Alistair's glass. "Now, are you ready to tell me what's troubling you? I can see you are not at all yourself, and I do believe that it's not all down to your illness." Alistair drank half of his replenished drink and still clutching the glass in both hands he turned to speak to Mortimer.

"May I ask, do you believe in the survival of the spirit beyond death?" said Alistair. He stared intensely at Mortimer in anticipation of his answer.

"The survival of the spirit after death? You are asking me whether or not I believe in ghosts?"

"Yes. Do you?"

"Well, as a man of the church I can say that I do believe that there is indeed an afterlife. I have been touched by many deaths Mr. Swift. I believe that the body is the chariot if you like within which the soul or spirit rides. When the body dies, and is buried, or cremated, the soul is lifted to heaven. To God."

"But do you believe that the spirit or soul can come back, or even to never enter heaven at all?" Mortimer drank some of his drink whilst he pondered the question Alistair had put to him.

"Well I believe that Jesus rose from the dead three days after his crucifixion. This means that his spirit was returned to his earthly body. So yes, I do. But why do you ask such a question?" Alistair finished his brandy before replying.

"The cavern outside, I went inside exploring. I found remains, the remains from what looks like an ancient burial. Three piles of rocks, graves. The Reverend Redgrave, he also found them. The bones he showed to you remember, you told me he showed you the bones!"

"Yes I told you, he became obsessed with what he had discovered. He intended to have them interred in the grounds of Saint. Peter."

"Yes, yes he did didn't he. I read his journal. I found it here, at the house. You see, from his journal it is clear that he was plagued also."

"Plagued? Whatever do you mean?"

"In the cavern, I found the remains, the same bones that Redgrave had studied, labelled, sketched . . ." Alistair began to cough and excused himself whilst he regained his composure. "The bones were all back inside the cavern, they still had the labels on. Redgrave . . . or something put Them back!"

"Something?"

"Yes, something. You see, I think I have disturbed something. Poking about in the cavern. And now it disturbs me." Mortimer rose to throw a log onto the fire. He stood a while watching the flames dance across the dry wood.

"You are telling me that you are being haunted. Is that right?"

"Yes. I believe that I am." Mortimer sat down again picking up his brandy.

"So what has happened to make you believe such a fantastic thing?"

"First it was the sounds, the breathing."

"Breathing?"

"Yes, a terrible sound, almost bestial. And then the gate. You see the thing, or phantom as I shall call it, it leaves the cave. I can hear the gate banging as it makes its way towards the house. I can hear it as I lie in bed. It taunts me with its hideous breathing." Alistair's hands began to shake and he placed his glass down next to the fireside. Mortimer watched as Alistair shook. He could not believe how the man he had first met a few days since had become this afraid, with almost a child-like fear searing through him.

"Mr. Swift, let us look at these things rationally shall we. First, you speak of a breathing sound. Would it not be fair to say that the wind could possibly have something to do with it? It has been incredibly windy these last few days. You are all alone and somewhat isolated here. It could be your Imagination playing with your mind. You also speak about the gate to the cavern banging. Again, I think the wind is the culprit. This is an old house after all, I know from my own experience how the wind can whip up about an old place like this, the wind can have many voices, moaning, whistling. You are the not the first person to imaging that they hear voices in the wind."

"I saw it!" Alistair retorted abruptly and he reached for the brandy bottle.

"You saw it? You mean you saw the . . . phantom?"

78

"Yes, tonight. Before you got here. It was in the house!" Alistair poured and drank down another large measure of spirit.

"So what exactly did you see?"

"I heard it at first. in the bedroom. I went to see. I saw . . . a shadow. I saw it move across the landing and down the stairs. It made no sound." Mortimer looked around the room in which they sat. He noticed the multitudes of candles burning brightly within an array of candlesticks, jam jars, and other receptacles.

"Tell me, do you have candles burning upstairs?"

"I do. Why?"

"Well there is the answer I think. The candles create shadows. In your present state of wellbeing you must have been suffering from fever induced hallucinations. A simple shadow created by the light of a candle, animated by the flickering flame. My dear fellow you are unwell." Alistair finished his drink and rose to stand on wobbly legs.

"Come with me. I want to show you something."

Mortimer and Alistair were in the master bedroom. Mortimer watched as Alistair fetched a bundle of sheets from the windowsill. He returned to where Mortimer stood and placed the bundle down on to the bed. "This was left for me to see." Gingerly, Alistair unfolded the bundle to reveal the gruesome contents. Mortimer leaned over to see the fleshy carcass, studded with blanket fluff.

"What in God's name is it?"

"It was my friend, my cat. Smokey."

"What happened to it?"

"It followed me into the cave. It never came out. I found this tonight left on my bed." Alistair looked up at Mortimer, he suddenly had the idea that Mortimer might be thinking that he carried out this awful deed. "It wasn't . . . I'd never . . . I never did it, if that's what you think?" Mortimer re-fastened the bundle and placed it onto a bedroom chair.

"Let's get you into bed old chap. We can talk about this in the morning. You need rest. Like I said I will stay here tonight. Make sure you are alright." Mortimer pulled back the bedsheets. Alistair removed his sweater and climbed inside.

"You don't believe me do you. You think I'm mad."

"I think you need a good night's rest. Like I said we can talk in the morning."

"Where will you sleep? I'm afraid the other bed isn't made up."

"Oh, don't worry, I shall make myself comfortable in that splendid armchair by your fireside. Now enough talking. Please get some rest." Alistair lay his head back on the pillow and closed his eyes. The effects of the brandy were beginning to take effect. Just as Mortimer was about to leave the room Alistair spoke.

"You will hear it too." He said. "If you listen, you will hear . . ." Alistair began to snore.

6

Alistair awoke and reached over to pick up his wristwatch. It was nine thirty. He had slept well. He sat up in bed. He could see the sun shining through the gap in the curtain. He got out of bed and pulled on his sweater, slipped his feet into his slippers. He coughed. His cough was a lot drier. He was starting to feel a little better. He became aware of an aroma drifting into his bedroom from the kitchen below. It was the smell of cooked bacon. His mouth began to water.

When Alistair entered the kitchen, he saw the Reverend Mortimer busily working over the wood stove. Mortimer was holding a frying pan containing plentiful rashes of bacon. There was a smaller pan that contained some sizzling fried eggs. A pot of coffee was steaming on top of the stove. Mortimer turned to greet Alistair.

"Good morning. I hope you slept well. I popped up to check on you this morning and you were sound asleep. I popped out to the town to buy some breakfast. You look as though you have some colour in your face. Are you feeling any better?"

"A little, yes thanks. You didn't have to go to all this trouble," said Alistair as he indicated the breakfast cooking on the stove.

"Well I thought I'd make sure you had eaten before I went to fetch a doctor."

"Oh, please, there's no need for a doctor, I will be fine. I'm actually feeling a lot better. I think my fever has broken," Alistair said before seating himself at the kitchen table.

"Well in my opinion I think you need assessment by a physician, and I can also make some enquiries regarding your power outage." Mortimer dished out the bacon and eggs and brought the breakfast over to the table. He then poured out two mugs of coffee before settling himself down to eat.

Alistair ate his breakfast greedily, and finished it quickly. He then sipped at his coffee before speaking. "I appreciate this. Thank you. You have been very kind."

"It's the least I could do. Did I mention that the snow has started to melt?"

"It has? Good. Without any transport, I find it practically impossible to make it into town. It's the incline!"

"Oh I know. Even in my old car I find it difficult. If it wasn't for the fact I have recently had a set of new tyres I wouldn't have been able to make it up and down myself." Alistair waited for Mortimer to finish his last bite of fried egg. Then he spoke again.

"Last night. Did you hear anything? See anything?" asked Alistair. Mortimer dabbed his mouth with a napkin and thought a moment before answering.

"You mean, did I experience anything supernatural? I definitely did not. And I do believe my friend, that now you are feeling better you will see how all of these troubles were nothing more than part of your affliction." Alistair drank some coffee before speaking again,

"Did I mention that I was a school teacher?"

"I think I do remember you saying something, you said you were retired from teaching. Is that right?"

"Yes. I used to teach history. I would never have described myself as particularly fanciful by nature. I am not one to suffer from an overactive imagination. What I told you last night really happened. I don't think that it was just part of my illness. Look, I have been fascinated by ancient times for as long as I can remember. Around the world the belief that we can survive the death of our bodies is extremely widespread. Ideas of the soul can be found in civilizations from ancient Egypt to the shamans of Siberia."

"I agree Mr. Swift, indeed most Christians, Muslims, and Hindus alive today believe that the soul can survive the physical body, but–" Alistair interrupted him,

"I believe what I heard, what I saw, what the Reverend Redgrave saw was real. Whatever we have disturbed by our lack of understanding and meddling is real. Somehow it now exists in an altered state. It is coherent and sentient. And I don't know what to do!" Alistair looked at Mortimer and Mortimer could see that there were tears in his eyes.

"What if I were to have a look in that cavern. I could have a poke around, see what's there. And when I find nothing would that help to ease your mind?"

"No. You mustn't go in there. But you could help me to close the gate. To fasten it again. To keep it inside!"

"It?"

"The phantom." Mortimer cleared away the breakfast plates and put them to rest inside the sink before returning to pour them both another coffee.

"I have decided to go into that cave Mr. Swift. If nothing else my curiosity has been roused beyond control. We could go in together if you like. We will find the answer to the sound of breathing you hear, and then yes I will help to fasten the gate."

"I really wouldn't want you to fall prey to the same fate as I."

"I won't Mr. Swift."

******

It was almost eleven o'clock in the morning by the time Mortimer and Alistair ventured outside. Mortimer had got the hurricane lamp working again and they made their way around the house to the cavern. When they reached the cave, Mortimer passed the hurricane lamp he was holding to Alistair. Alistair took the lamp and Mortimer fiddled with the gate, opening and closing it. "You see, the gate swings loosely, the land falls away from it and has created a slope. Although it opens inwards, the wind could easily push against it causing it to thrash against its post here see?" Mortimer demonstrated using his walking cane to push at the gate. Alistair was not convinced. He looked around, studying the snow on the ground.

"You see those?" he said pointing at a trail of footprints in the snow leading back towards the house. "That's the trail the phantom made. During its night visits." Mortimer scanned the trail for a moment.

"How can you be sure that you yourself didn't make this trail?"

"The snow had freshly fallen. When I saw it, I hadn't been near." Mortimer studied both Alistair and again the trail in the snow.

"You know an animal could have made this trail. A fox, or badger perhaps?"

"What, those prints are man sized. My feet are a size ten, and those prints dwarf my own!"

"You know, I once read somewhere that the wind can widen a snow print from an animal as small as a squirrel and make it large enough as though it had been made by a person. The snow gradually caves in from around the edge of the print, the wind scoops it out, then the process begins again until you are left with what we see here. Do you see?"

"Not really. There was no wind at the time. Not as far as I remember. Look Reverend, I don't think you should go in," said Alistair.

"Will you come with me?" asked Mortimer. Alistair shook his head,

"I fear it. I am sorry you must think me a complete fool!"

"Not a fool. We all have our fears Mr. Swift," spoke Mortimer. He took back the lamp from Alistair and Alistair held the gate open for him whilst he slipped through.

******

The Reverend Mortimer had travelled half the way down the passage leading to the chamber when he spotted Alistair's discarded candelabra. Bending down he leaned the candelabra against the rock wall and pocketed the candles that had fallen out. He thought Alistair could do with all the candles he could get until his power was back on.

A little further along Mortimer stopped to examine some wall art. The painting was primitive and depicted what appeared to be the transformation of a stick man first into a stag, then finally into a bird. Underneath the painting was a stencilled hand feature. Mortimer conjectured that if primitive man had no written language as such, then he would be inclined to sign a picture with a reproduction of his own hand.

Moving onwards Mortimer entered the main chamber. He held up the paraffin lamp so that he could take in the splendour of the ceiling to the chamber. The soda straws and stalactites were indeed a wondrous spectacle. Once he had grown tired at marvelling at the chamber ceiling he cast his lamp towards the ground. A little way ahead of him he could make out the three rock piles.

Where these the graves that Redgrave and Swift had talked about, he wondered.

The floor around the graves was littered with torn shreds of cardboard. Mortimer noticed a small yellow and green box lying between the second and third grave. He picked it up. It was a box of matches. He slipped them into his pocket along with the candles.

He continued to walk between the two graves until he had reached the wall behind them. He held up his lamp to study more stencilled hand prints. He wondered how old they must be. Hundreds of thousands of years perhaps. Yet they looked as new and as fresh as though they had been done only today.

He traced one of the prints using his index finger then stopped when his finger tip felt moist. He held his hand near to the lamp. He could see his fingertip was red, the same red as the hand stencil. The wall must be damp, he thought. The wet was causing the pigment to become reconstituted and to stick to whatever touched it. He cleaned his finger on his trousers before walking back through the graves and stopping at the front end of them. He noticed that some of the stones on one of the graves were splattered with a red substance. As he held the lamp near to the end pile of stones he saw something poking through them. It looked like a piece of grey fur.

Removing some of the rocks, Mortimer released the piece of fur. He held it up to examine in front of the lamp. It was the whole skin of a cat, complete with face and ears. In repulsion, he tossed it down behind the graves. The skin at first slapped coldly onto the rocks before unfurling slowly and exposing its wet, bloody underside as it slid into an untidy heap on the floor.

At this point Mortimer thought that he heard a low rhythmic breathing. He stood completely still and strained his ears. He held out the lamp as he listened. This time there was only silence. He continued to walk around the chamber.

Outside the cavern, Alistair was getting worried. He glanced at the clock on his wrist. Mortimer had been inside the cave for a good thirty minutes, and still there was no sign of him returning. Alistair walked through the gate and stood at the entrance to the cavern. He peered into the dark mouth but it gave up none of its secrets. A loud 'kaah-kaah' erupted from behind him. He spun around and saw the pitchy raven perched on top of the monolith opposite. Not wanting to turn his back on the raven but also eager to see the return of the Reverend Mortimer, he cupped his hands to his mouth and called for Mortimer several times. The raven sat still. Watching.

Soon Alistair could hear a shuffling sound coming from within the cave. He placed a hand over his eyes and peered inside. Still he could discern nothing. The shambling grew louder. There was something glinting in the darkness of the tunnel before him, then Alistair saw the familiar form of Mortimer, he was carrying the silver candelabra as he made his way towards the exit.

Once outside, Mortimer dusted himself down and tapped his cane against the wall of the cavern to remove the remnants of the dirt from the cavern floor. "Well, that certainly is quite a unique experience. Yes, quite unusual indeed," said Mortimer. He handed the candelabra to Alistair, "Yours I imagine?" he said. Alistair nodded. "These too I expect?" Mortimer reached into his pocket and pulled out a box of matches. Alistair took them from his hand, and smiled,

"Yes, I lost them. Tried to find them. Failed miserably I'm afraid," he said.

"I saw the graves. And you say that the bones collected by Redgrave have been replaced under the rocks?"

"Yes, I removed some rocks and was able to see them."

"I wonder how they got back there? Did Redgrave somehow put them back?" mused Mortimer.

"Maybe he didn't," replied Alistair.

"Oh you think the phantom replaced them? Well we have both had our discussion on whether or not we believe in the possibility of the continuation of the spirit beyond the demise of the flesh. I think if spirits do exist, they certainly don't have enough substance to be able to move rocks, or even to stomp out a trail through snow. For some reason, Redgrave must have returned them. But he was so adamant that they should be interred at the church."

"Did you see anything else, hear anything at all?" said Alistair, and he looked at Mortimer hoping for something, anything that could affirm the confirmation of his own sanity.

"I did, I saw some remarkable prehistoric paintings. Wonderful geological features. But nothing preternatural I'm afraid," Mortimer added before holding the gate open for Alistair to walk through. Mortimer closed the gate behind them both. "Now, I suggest the easiest method of fixing this gate closed is by tying it so. Do you have any rope?" Alistair thought a moment,

"I think I saw some in the workshop," he said.

******

With the gate securely fastened using rope that Mortimer and Alistair had found in the workshop, both men were back inside the house. A fresh pot of coffee sat on the table between them. Mortimer spoke again about fetching a doctor to Alistair. Alistair refused, "that really will not be necessary, you see I have decided to leave this old place."

"Leave? You mean sell up?" asked Mortimer somewhat shocked.

"Yes exactly. I can't stay here. Not now. I will put Olde Tudor back on the market."

"But where will you go?"

"I will stay with my sister Gwen, just until I have completely sorted out my affairs. I will pack tonight and leave in the morning."

"I see." Mortimer finished his coffee and opened the lid of the coffee pot only to see that it was now empty.

"I was wondering, and I realise that I have taken enough liberties already with your kindness and generosity, but could I impose on you one final time and ask for a lift to the station tomorrow?"

"Why of course. If you are certain that you have made up your mind."

"Yes I have. Thank you. Shall we say around nine?"

"Of course. I shall be here at nine. I will still telephone around to see if I can get your power reconnected. The prospect of you spending another night at this place without lights and a telephone worries me."

"Thank you. But I should be fine. I am feeling much better now, and if I busy myself later with packing, the night will not be a long one!"

******

The night drew in quickly as always. Alistair had managed to pack all his most essential belongings together. He had packed all his clothes into a large brown Leather-trimmed, brass buckled suitcase. He had no way of letting Gwen know of his intentions to spend time with her at her house, but hoped the surprise would be a pleasant one.

With a multitude of candles lit around the house, and a quarter bottle of brandy resting on the small table by the fire, he settled down to continue to read the journal of the late George Redgrave. Even though he had decided to leave

Olde Tudor, he wanted to try to understand more about the unsettling events he had suffered since occupying the house.

There were only a few torn pages remaining, clinging on by the thinnest of threads used to sew the book into its binding. The Reverend's words seemed to have been added with a trembling hand.

I know not what this creature is, or from whence it came. But it would appear to have my scent, and a desire to instil fear in my heart and soul. What it wants, I can only guess. I was certain at first that it was the disembodied spirit of one of the relics from the cave. Now I am not so sure. It could be a tutelary deity, a guardian spirit put in place during ancient times to watch over this plot. I believe this place was once thought of as a sacred site. And I believe it is defended at all costs. I have asked the Lord God by way of prayer for protection and release from this ordeal. Why does he not help me, his deputy in the cloth? The Lord God, the father is the almighty, the supreme being. His house and his laws over which I am the current upholder is the one true holy place, not some foetid cavern. I shall inter the bones at St. Peter. Once buried in holy soil this deity, this guardian will fade and diminish and become little more than a faint whispery echo on the wind. I must do it. I must find the strength and the courage to do it.

Alistair closed the book. There were no more words by Redgrave. He poured himself a large glass of brandy and stared at the flames in the hearth. He wondered had Redgrave managed to bury the bones, would he still be alive today?

After two more glasses of brandy Alistair rose unsteadily from his seat. He went over to the nearest window and parted the curtains a little. Bravely he peered outside into the dark. The snow was still providing nocturnal effulgence that made the night not so murky.

There was nothing untoward outside for a change he thought. No disconcerting breathing, or rattling gates. All he had to do was survive this one last night and then he would be gone. He would rid himself of this ordeal.

Not wanting to sleep upstairs, Alistair wedged a broom handle under the handle of the door leading to the garden, the cavern. He plumped up a cushion and set himself to rest in a chair by the fire. He would spend the night like this he thought. In no time, the brandy had made him sleepy and he slipped into a malady free slumber.

******

The Reverend John Mortimer steered his black Rover 75 around the bend and began to apply the brakes as Olde Tudor came into view at the bottom of the lane. He brought his car to a stop just outside the gate. When he climbed out of his car he was aware of the smell of fire. He glanced up at the chimney on the roof but it was dormant. It was then he noticed a plume of grey smoke rising from the back of the house.

Mortimer found Alistair standing near to a large tin can. The can was burning with a fierce fire. "Morning," Mortimer shouted. Alistair looked up and greeted the Reverend.

"Good morning. My goodness is it nine already?" he glanced at his wrist watch.

"Yes indeed. But don't hurry. I have little else to do this morning. I am glad to find you looking more robust!" said Mortimer as he came over to inspect what Alistair was burning. Alistair used a long stick to poke at the fire.

"It's the cat. I couldn't just leave it there, in the house. Ground was still too hard to dig. I thought this was a cleaner method."

"Indeed," replied Mortimer, "Are you all packed?"

"Almost. Just a couple of bits and pieces left. I can throw them into a bag. It shouldn't take very long. Would you like to come inside? There's a little coffee left on the stove." Mortimer gladly accepted the offer of some warm coffee, and he noticed that all the while Alistair was speaking, he was always glancing around himself as though looking for something high in the trees.

Mortimer sat himself at the kitchen table whilst Alistair set his bags down near the front door. Soon Alistair came to inform Mortimer that he was ready to leave and the pair of them loaded the bags into the boot on the Rover. Again, Mortimer noticed how Alistair scanned the skies as they packed the luggage. Soon the Car was pulling away and climbing up the steep hill into the town.

As the car drove carefully through the slushy residue from the recent snow pile, Mortimer spoke, "how was your last night at the house?"

"Oh, not so bad. I packed, and then I must admit, I indulged myself of perhaps too much brandy. I slept well, although I have a slight crick in my neck from falling to sleep in a fireside Chair!"

"Well, I expect you will enjoy a good sleep at your sister's house tonight," replied Mortimer.

"Yes. I am looking forward to it immensely. May I ask another favour?"

"Of course. What is it?"

"Before we go to the station, would you mind dropping me off at the property agents on the high street, Brierly and sons?"

"Why of course. Would you like me to wait whilst you clear up your business?"

"If you could that would be jolly decent of you, it shouldn't take me long."

When Alistair entered the office of the younger Brierly, he found Jacob clearing up some business with another client. Alistair hovered in front of the fire in the room and waited for Jacob to see his client out of the office. Jacob looked a little irritated at the sudden appearance of Alistair in his office.

When they were both alone Jacob spoke first, "I'm sorry, did we have an appointment?" Alistair removed his hat before replying,

"No, I'm afraid I was unable to make one. I have been trapped in my home the last week," he said.

Jacob sat down offering Alistair a chair at the other side of the desk.

"Mr Swift, isn't it? I thought I recognised you. You purchased the old house at the bottom of the lane, didn't you?"

"Yes, that's right," Alistair replied with an angry tone to his voice. Jacob looked over Alistair. He noted how pale he looked, and how he had such dark circles around his eyes as though somebody had taken two lumps of coal from the scuttle by the fire and rubbed them into his eye sockets.

"Well, what can we do for you today Mr Swift?"

"I would like to sell Olde Tudor."

"Selling? Already?"

"Indeed I am," spoke Alistair, never taking his eyes from Jacob's.

"Well to be perfectly honest, you have surprised me. If you don't mind me asking, what is the reason behind the decision to sell?" Alistair continued to stare at Jacob before he spoke again,

"I think you know why," he said softly.

"I'm afraid you have me at a disadvantage Mr. Swift, I can assure you that."

"You knew about the house. It was something you said to me when I first came here. If my memory is correct, after I mentioned that I was a retired school teacher, you said, if I may quote you, *a man with his feet firmly on the ground. Not open to fanciful leanings.* Now, why would you say that before showing me the details of Olde Tudor?" Jacob looked down at his desk, the penetrating stare form Alistair's red, bloodshot eyes was overbearing.

"Look Mr. Swift, I can assure you I don't know what you mean, I–"

"Lies. You knew about that house, or more to the point, you knew about the problems that would befall anyone who had the misfortune to live there!" at this point, Alistair had removed a handkerchief and was now mopping his brow. He hoped it was the warmness of the room that was causing him to perspire. "Please, Mr. Brierly, don't pretend you don't know. How many others has this happened to?" Jacob pressed his fingertips together as he sat back into his seat.

"Rumours, just silly rumours, that's all. Old houses have voices so they say."

"Voices?" Alistair's voice was now raised sufficiently enough to alert the senior Mr Brierly, Arthur, who came rushing into Jacob's office. He stood in the open doorway before speaking to his son.

"Jacob, is there a problem?" Jacob leaned forward in his chair before answering his father,

"No, it's fine. Mr Swift here was unhappy with his purchase of the old Tudor house, we were discussing getting it back on the market. It's quite alright Dad." Arthur Brierly continued to linger and watch Alistair wipe his brow whilst rocking agitated in his chair. "Isn't that right Mr Swift?" continued Jacob. Alistair rose from his seat and pocketed his handkerchief.

"I will leave it with you, to begin proceedings. I-I will be in touch next week to see how things are progressing," Alistair said and he replaced his trilby and made for the exit. When he had left the building, Arthur turned to Jacob and said,

"We're going to have trouble selling that old place. Does he know?"

"Yes Dad, he knows," answered Jacob.

Outside the property agency Alistair climbed back into the Reverend Mortimer's car. "Everything sorted?" asked Mortimer. Alistair nodded,

"Yes, thank you. You were very kind to wait. Now, I think I should make my train," he glanced at his wristwatch, "just!" Mortimer put his car into gear then pulled away down station road.

7

As the train approached Cromer, Alistair removed his suitcase from the overhead rack and made his way to the doors. He noticed that the snow was still hanging around in the corners of the station platform. He buttoned his overcoat as high as it would go, donned his hat, and adjusted his scarf.

It was almost midday yet his breath still left a vapour cloud in front of him as he waited for the next empty taxicab. Whilst he waited in the carpark behind the station, he watched a pair of seagulls as they milled about on the platform, gingerly picking up and then dropping spent cigarette butts as they searched for tasty morsels. He breathed in a lung full of cool air then coughed a dry cough. His breathing had improved, in fact, he was feeling a whole lot better than he did only a couple of days since.

A black taxicab pulled into the carpark, its sign was lit indicating that it was ready for the next fayre. Alister approached the taxi and the driver climbed out and put Alistair's suitcase in the boot. Soon he was on his way to Gwen's country house in west Runton.

During transit he decided that he would not go into any detail regarding his ill fortune with Olde Tudor. He would simply explain to Gwen that the place was not quite right for him, and that he would rather find somewhere in Runton.

Somewhere not far from the coast so that he could be of help to her whenever she needed it.

Alistair asked the driver to stop a little distance from where Gwen's house sat. He wanted to walk the final few yards, to take in the countryside. He wanted to make sure that he could settle here, to feel at home.

As he approached Gwen's house he could see that she had been busy, there was a line of washing blowing gently in the breeze. Her front garden however was somewhat overgrown with bramble and nettle. The old sycamore, that at one point had been struck dead by lightening, was leaning even more precariously towards the house than the last time he had seen it. He would help her to sort out the garden he thought as he made his way up the old brick path to the porch.

Gwen had been delighted to see her brother standing on the doorstep. After some brief affectionate greetings, he had partially explained his mishap with buying Olde Tudor and asked if he could stay with her until his affairs had been dealt with. Gwen was more than happy to have him stay and she began to get a room ready for him as he unpacked.

Later in the afternoon, Alistair had made a pot of tea whilst Gwen dished them both a bowl of lamb stew she had prepared earlier. They sat down to eat as dark began to creep in outside. For the first time in days, Alistair need not fear the night drawing in, he was a long way from the cave here he thought to himself as he ate the delicious meal in front of him.

Gwen studied her brother as he ate. He looked thinner in the face. His whole countenance was changed somewhat and she decided to question him. "Ally, I hope you don't mind me saying this, but you don't look at all yourself!" Alistair stopped slurping at his spoon of stew and looked up at Gwen. He then placed his spoon down into his bowl and dabbed his mouth with a napkin.

"I have been a little under the weather, caught a rook that's all," he said. Gwen frowned as she answered him,

"what on earth do you mean? Caught a rook?" Alistair suddenly realised what he'd said and wondered why he chose that phrase, perhaps subconsciously.

"Oh, sorry Gwen. It's an idiom I picked up in Thornbarrow. I think it means to catch a cold!" he explained.

"I see. But you look so pale. And your eyes look terrible. Are you sure it was just a cold?"

"Yes, nothing more serious, I assure you."

"You need to take better care of yourself," Gwen paused a moment whilst she thought about the next thing she was about to say, "isn't it time you started seeing someone again. No man is an island you know. You need someone who can take care of you, you don't intend to be a bachelor for the rest of your life do you?" Alistair shook his head,

"of course not Gwen, but I'm no youngster you know."

"Oh, go on with you! You might have retired early, but you're not over the hill yet."

"I'm beginning to feel it sometimes. But it's not just that." Alistair finished the last of his stew and poured himself and Gwen another cup of tea from the pot.

"It's Evelyn isn't it. You'd feel guilty, if you were to be with someone else. I understand. I miss my Jack so much," Gwen stopped talking to glance over at a small silver framed oval picture of a uniformed air force pilot whose beaming smile below a thin moustache almost spoke to her. Alistair reached across the table and gave Gwen's hand a little squeeze,

"Yes, you're right. I do miss her, she was the one Gwen, she really was. I can't even contemplate, you know. Someone else." Gwen nodded, she was trying too hard to swallow a lump in her throat to answer him properly. She dabbed at her eyes with a napkin. "But I turn your comment back at you Gwen, your no old maid either. You could still fall in love, have a family. All those things. We don't have to both live under the shadow of the war for the rest of our lives." Gwen smiled as though to say he was right and she began to collect up the dinner plates and bowls. Alistair helped. "Tomorrow I thought I'd help tidy up the front garden a little, looks more overgrown than I last remembered," Alistair said as he carried a large pot of leftover stew into the kitchen.

"Oh, don't worry about the garden, you don't have to do that. Have a holiday. You look as though you need it," she said as she began to wash the dishes whilst Alistair dried them using a tea towel.

"No Gwen, I must make myself useful. Still not used to being retired you know. And that tree, well, I'm surprised it's still standing!"

Alistair withdrew to his bedroom at around midnight. The curtains were open and he glanced outside. The moon was big and almost full again. The dead sycamore was leaning close to his window. It reminded him of the large ash in the grounds of Olde Tudor and how he could not bear to look at the shadow it had cast behind those old worn drapes for fear of seeing something terrible climbing through its boughs. He closed the curtains.

Once into his pyjamas, Alistair turned down the bedsheets and ran a poker through the glowing coals in the small fireplace to liven it up. He then removed his suitcase from under the bed and unbuckled it. He had packed a few documents relating to the purchase of Olde Tudor that he intended to post back to Brierly and Sons. He left them on the dresser.

Before he replaced the suitcase back under the bed he saw the old journal of the Reverend Redgrave half peeking out from a pocket in the lid of the case. He removed it and held it in his hands. He had no idea why he had packed it. He had read everything within. Maybe, it was so he could read Redgrave's words so that they could reassure him that he had not become temporarily insane during his short residence at Olde Tudor.

He walked over to the fireplace and cast the journal onto the rekindled coals. He stood and watched it bubble and crack and fold shut like a drawn purse as the yellow flames licked hungrily around its edges. He stood and watched until the only thing left of it was a small pile of black layered powder, almost wafer-like. "Ashes to ashes," he muttered to himself before climbing into bed.

******

Next morning Alistair was up early and tackling the overgrown clumps of bramble in Gwen's front garden. He had found an old billhook and fixed it to a broken broom handle. He used this tool to hack at the thick stems of the bramble, he had managed to clear quite a lot of it before Gwen emerged from the house wearing a coat and pushing Alistair's old bicycle. She leaned the bike against a wall before turning to speak, "Ally, I'm going into town to get some bread and bits and pieces. Is there anything I can get for you whilst I'm there?" Alistair stopped working and hung the billhook from a low branch on the sycamore,

"Are you going near the sea front?"

"I wasn't, but I can if you like. May I take your bicycle? To be honest I've been using it since you left it here, the basket is useful."

"Of course you can. If you do go to the sea front, pick me up some of that dressed crab they do from the little blue house, the one you showed me last time remember? It was delicious."

"I will. Oh, and Ally, don't work too hard, you've been sick remember. You need a rest," she said as she wheeled the bicycle out through the gate. Alistair took a break.

Leaning against the sycamore he watched his sister as she threw her leg up and over the back wheel then plopped herself down on the saddle pushing herself off along the lane as though she'd ridden that bike her whole life. Taking a handkerchief from out his pocked, he wiped his brow, it was heavy work and although the air was still cool, he had worked up a sweat.

Kaah-kaah! A cry rang out above his head. He dropped his handkerchief and retrieved his billhook. That sound instilled deep fear within him, a sound he had not heard since . . . kaah-kaah! the shrill call came again. He turned and scanned the fields around the house, searching. He saw nothing. Slowly he backed towards the house. It then came for him, kaah-kaah!

A black quilled living dart, shot down from the top branches of the sycamore. Its feet, like a pair of barbed spurs scraped across his scalp drawing blood. Instinctively, he swished the billhook around himself, hoping to catch whatever was trying to attack him before he could cast his eyes upon it. kaah-kaah! Glancing upwards, he saw the black, hooded form of a raven perched high atop the dead tree, the sooty scorch marks borne from a thunderbolt were its perfect camouflage.

Alistair picked up a fist sized stone from near the gravel path that led to the front door. He took aim at the bird and bowled the stone. As ever the bird was off its perch and soaring aloft before the stone could mark it. Alistair watched as it climbed ever higher, and circled like a vulture, riding the thermal currents until his eyes could no longer perceive it.

Inside the house Alistair was still bathing his grazed headwound with a flannel cloth when Gwen returned. She carried in some shopping without looking at him and went into the kitchen. She spoke as she began to fill the pantry, "I got you the crab Ally, oh, and I posted the letter you left by the front door, you wanted it posted, didn't you?"

"Yes, thanks," replied Alistair, he came into the kitchen with a flannel pressed to his head. Gwen was alarmed when she saw the once white cloth reddened with her brother's blood.

"Goodness! What happened to you?"

"Oh, I, I caught my head, on some thorns. It'll be alright," he said thinking it best not to elaborate too much, he didn't think that she would actually believe that he was being pursued and relentlessly attacked by a malicious raven.

"Are you sure? Let me take a look I can–"

"I'm fine Gwen, really. It's stopped bleeding now."

"Well you remember Aunt Lilly, she died from pricking her hand on a rose bush, you shouldn't–"

"I've cleaned it well, I'll be fine, please don't fuss. Shall I prepare some of that crabmeat?" Alistair went off into the kitchen, Gwen followed him in,

"I can cut us up some bread to go with it, it's freshly baked today and still warm."

"That'll be nice." Gwen started slicing the bread,

"Oh, I was listening to the wireless this morning. Apparently, we're to have a blood moon tonight, whatever that is." Alistair carefully dished up the crabmeat onto two small plates,

"a blood moon is a total lunar eclipse. During the eclipse, all the sunlight is blocked from the moon by the earth, well most of it is. Some of the sunlight is refracted through the earth's shadow, and that gives it the red colour."

"Gosh Ally, how do you know all that stuff? I suppose, being a teacher . . ."

"Well I had to teach the boys something you know, although frankly, that was my colleague, Davenport's field. He taught science." Alistair carried the crabmeat to the dining table, Gwen had already set down the freshly cut bread.

During the evening Alistair and Gwen talked about the old days, when they lived with their parents in Norwich. They reminisced about school days, and the games they'd played in the streets once the school day was over. They both listened to the light programme from the BBC on the wireless before deciding to retire to bed.

Alistair sat on the end of his bed. He thought about the raven that had attacked him early in the day and he went over to the dressing cabinet to examine his scalp in the mirror.

He noticed that the new wound was almost superimposed across the scar of his previous injury. He wondered if it was indeed the same bird, or did all ravens in this part of the country have a propensity to attack middle aged men. He shook off the thought that the bird may not be a bird at all. The thought that it might in some way be a sentinel, sent out by whatever spectre had undertaken the charge of protecting that fusty cavern was not a pleasant notion.

As he began to draw the curtains he noticed the large full moon hanging silently in the starry sky. Its colour was like oxidised iron. There was something about the colour of the moon that unsettled him. Remembering the dreams triggered by his recent fever, he pulled the curtains tight and climbed into bed.

Alistair had a troubled sleep. He woke many times feeling as though he had just broken free of a nightmare, but he couldn't remember anything of the dream, only the feeling of mortal dread that the dreaming had bestowed upon him.

The sixth and final time he woke, he found himself paralysed, unable to move. It was as though his wrists and ankles had been tethered to the bed. He struggled, but his leaden arms and legs would not move. Then he heard it.

At first the low, grunting, breathing seemed to be a distant call from somewhere far away outside of the house. As he focused on the noise, the all so familiar disturbing noise, he was horrified to realise that the breathing originated from within the room.

With his eyes tightly shut and in absolute fear, he felt the blanket being pulled with force from off his body. He opened his eyes, and found himself not to be lying on his bed but tied to a stone slab. The bindings were so tight they were cutting into the flesh of his arms and feet. He blinked several times trying to clear the vision, but it made no difference, he remained strapped at the centre of a stone circle.

The red effulgence from the blood moon tinted the tall standing stones that surrounded him. The same red light picked out the scowls worn on the faces of the primitive looking crowd of men, women, and children who were slowly advancing towards him.

Alistair tried to scream, but his voice was muted. Unable to move he winced as the first strike of a flint scored down his thigh. Then came another. The pain he felt with each cut seemed to snap him out of his ethereal vision of being tethered inside a long-forgotten monolith ring. He was now back inside his bedroom but the assault continued.

Unable to see what was attacking him, he could hear a grinding cracking noise created by his indiscernible assailant as it moved around his bed, invisible. The low guttural breathing from this creature grew louder with every strike of sharp stone. Alistair found his voice and screamed.

Gwen was awakened by the desperate cries from her brother. She quickly threw her dressing gown around her shoulders and ran across the landing to Alistair's bedroom.

She gripped the bedroom door handle and pushed, but the door seemed to be locked. "Ally, Ally what's wrong? Ally open the door!" Alistair replied only with more fearful cries. Gwen twisted the handle some more and kicked at the door, she was relieved when it opened.

Quickly she flicked on the light and saw her brother writhing in a gore soaked bed, blood oozing from under his pyjamas. The sight of Gwen broke his paralysis, "it came for me! My god it came for me here!"

******

Alistair was still shaking as Gwen tried to clean his wounds. She was no nurse, but she knew that the wounds on his legs and arms needed sutures. She carried a bowl of bloodied water out to the kitchen sink and poured it away, she returned with a large glass of brandy for Alistair.

The brandy calmed him, reducing his trembling. Gwen parted the curtains in the sitting room and glanced out. Dawn had broken. There was no sign yet of Phillip Renshaw, the local doctor. Gwen had called Phillip after she had calmed and settled Alistair in the sitting room. Alistair had pleaded for her not to call a doctor but she would not listen to his appeals.

As they both sat and listened quietly to the dawn chorus outside, Alistair began to speak about what happened to him, not only at Gwen's house, but also about the events back at Olde Tudor.

Gwen listened but grew concerned for her brother's state of mind. She couldn't understand why he would believe in such follies. He was a teacher, she had always been proud of his achievements, her brother was clever. Now he looked broken as he babbled about ghosts and phantoms. Listening to him though seemed to ease his anxiety and reduce his agitation.

"At first, I thought I was imagining things, but everything that I heard, I felt was all corroborated. I found the journal you see, the Reverend Redgrave. He lived in Olde Tudor, he was also . . . plagued." Gwen listened and thought she would try to help her brother realise that maybe all of this was down to his recent sickness.

"Where is this journal Ally, are you sure that whatever was written in it was factual, I mean the reverend may have been writing fiction, and when you were sick you—"

"No, no you don't understand. I heard, saw, I-I . . ."

"Ally, you told me you were sick. When I saw you turn up at my doorstep I thought my goodness! You looked terrible." Alistair finished the remains of the brandy in his glass,

"You sound just like Mortimer,"

"Who?"

"A friend, he helped me. Helped me when—" Alistair was cut short. A loud rapping on the front door caused him to recoil in fear, "Don't open the door Gwen, it's, it's . . . that . . . thing. It's come for me!" Gwen rose from her seat, it pained her to see Alistair almost crying like a frightened child.

"That will be Doctor Renshaw, I have to let him in." Alistair gripped her hand tightly, so tightly it hurt her. She carefully pulled her hand out of his, "Don't worry, he will help you. It'll be alright."

Gwen opened the door and the doctor stepped inside removing his hat. Doctor Renshaw was tall with brown hair side-parted neatly. He wore round wire rimmed spectacles and carried a leather physician's bag. Gwen took the doctor's hat and coat and led him over to where Alistair sat, curled on a seat in almost a foetal position. The doctor pulled up a chair and sat beside him.

A brief explanation from Gwen about how she had found her brother the previous night was given to the doctor. The doctor began to examine Alistair, he looked at his eyes and his throat. He felt around Alistair's neck and listened to his chest using a stethoscope. Finally, the doctor began to examine the wounds on his legs and arm.

Alistair had his pyjama sleeve rolled up exposing the flap of loose skin and red bloody tissue beneath. His legs were similarly exposed. Gwen went to the kitchen to make a pot of tea. She could hear the doctor and Alistair talking but she was not able to discern the exact nature of the conversation. When she had returned, she saw that the doctor had applied bandages to Alistair's wounds.

She handed the doctor a cup of tea that he took with gratitude, "Thank you Gwen, my first cuppa of the day!" Gwen smiled uneasily whilst the doctor drank some of his tea, she wondered what he would tell her about Alistair.

When he finished drinking, the doctor replaced some items into his bag and clasped it shut, "is there anywhere we can go for a quiet word?" he said. Gwen nodded and led him into the kitchen. "Your brother has wounds that I believe were self-inflicted, perhaps using a razor. Has he been under any strain lately?" Gwen shook her head,

"Not really, I don't think so. He recently bought a house that he had some trouble with, I'm not sure I fully understand the nature of the problem he had, but he was recently sick with a fever."

"Yes, he mentioned the fever. I had a look at him, he seems to be generally over it, however his glands are still a little large. What your brother needs is rest Gwen. He looks as though he has been suffering anxiety problems. Has anxiety been a problem for him previously?" Gwen thought a moment before answering,

"No, not as far I can remember. He recently retired from his work as a school teacher."

"I wonder why he did that Gwen. He is still some way off the usual retirement age if you see what I mean."

"Hmm, yes I know. He said that the war had taken all the best pupils. And after the death of his fiancée, his heart just was not in teaching anymore, I think."

"Well like I said he needs rest, and plenty of it. I have left him with some pills, see that he starts taking them once per day, they should help with his anxiety. If he needs more when he's finished you know where to find me, and oh yes, those wounds will need stitching. They're pretty deep you know, he ought to go to the hospital. I will call around in a few days to see how things are going."

Gwen thanked the doctor and watched as he drove his car back towards Cromer sea front. She closed the door and was about to start preparing both herself and Alister some breakfast when Alister grabbed her hand as she went by, "has he gone?" he asked. Gwen nodded,

"He left you some pills, he said you need to get those wounds seen to, we should get you to the hospital."

"No Gwen, I'm not going to no hospital. I need to go back!"

"Back?"

"Yes, back to Olde Tudor. There is something I simply must do, to rid myself of it."

"It?" Gwen said. She looked at Alistair's eyes, there was a glaze to them that made him look a little crazy. "You can't go back there, the doctor said you needed rest. Whatever happened to you back there, I don't pretend to understand, but it made you sick, made you–"

"Made me what Gwen? Made me cut myself? Is that what you think happened? Is that what the doctor told you?" Gwen couldn't look at him anymore, she couldn't stand to see him act in this wild and bizarre manner. "I need to go back. If I don't, I will never be rid of it don't you see? I will never be rid of it!" Gwen picked up the bottle of pills the doctor had left and held them out for Alistair,

"here take one of these, they might help." Alistair knocked the bottle out of Gwen's hand, it hit the floor hard and rolled along the rug ending up out of sight beneath an armchair.

"I don't need those, they will not help me. If anything, they will render me senseless and at the mercy of the terror that stalks me." Gwen started to cry,

"Ally, I just want to help you. Please stay here, do what the doctor says," she sobbed. Alistair stood up, he winced as the muscles flexed behind his wounded thigh, blood had already began darkening through the bandage.

"I have to fight it Gwen, if I don't the same fate will befall me as it did Redgrave. Redgrave had the answer I think. He wanted to bury them, bury them on consecrated ground. That is what I must do, I must bury the bones Gwen, bury them at Saint. Peter."

******

Gwen had finished preparing Alistair a pack lunch; she had put it into a small tin box with an apple. He came downstairs carrying his suitcase, this time he had packed lightly, only one change of clothes. The rest of the room in the case had been taken up with candles, matches, and the two torches that Gwen owned. He set the case down by the front door. "I called you a taxi cab, should be here in a few minutes," Gwen said as she watched him carefully pull his coat on over his sore arm.

"Thanks, I left the telephone number of the house on the bedroom dresser, hopefully the place has been reconnected by now. I also left the number of Saint Peter, the reverend Mortimer is a friend, if you can't reach me for whatever reason call him."

"I will. Oh Ally, can I not convince you to stay here?"

"Only if you should see me dead Gwen. I'm doing this to save my life!"

"Then let me come with you. I can help you do what you think needs to be done!"

"I couldn't do that, not to you. You would also become . . . contaminated. No Gwen this is my curse not yours."

"But what about your wounds, the doctor said they needed stitching. They might get infected."

"No, I watched him clean them up pretty good, I think I'll be alright. I will go straight to the hospital when I return."

"You will? Do you promise me?"

"I promise, I really do." There was a short honk of vehicle horn outside.

"That will be the taxi. Take care of yourself," Gwen said as she fetched him his hat. Alistair nodded and they briefly hugged before he turned and opened the door.

Alistair stepped outside and before he walked down the path to the waiting taxi cab, he cautiously glanced upwards, scanning the skies, then the trees, then the bushes. Satisfied that he could make the distance without any further trouble he hobbled towards the waiting driver who was now out of the vehicle and opening the boot in preparation for stowing away Alistair's luggage. Gwen's heart sank as she watched the taxi pull away, for some reason she had the nagging feeling it might be the last time she would see her brother.

******

The ride to the station was short. Alistair, now back on the train heading to Thornbarrow sat thoughtful. Maybe Gwen was right. How was he going to do what he had to do, what he feared the most? How was he going to find the strength to enter that cavern knowing all the time what could be waiting for him, watching him enter from somewhere deep inside, within the darkness.

He wondered if it even knew what was in his thoughts. Did it know his plan, to bury the bones as Redgrave intended? Would it be waiting for him, would it be setting traps for him to prevent him from doing it? Alistair dreaded what lay before him. He contemplated asking Mortimer for assistance, but if things went wrong he would be condemning Mortimer to a similar fate. He simply could not inflict this upon someone who had shown him only friendship.

The brakes on the wheels of the train squealed as it slowly pulled into the station. Alistair read the platform signs for Thornbarrow as they glided past his window. Already there were groups of eager travellers approaching the train carriages as the train ground to a stop.

The train guards opened the doors as people stepped off and onto the train. A guard helped Alistair with his suitcase, as Alistair had lifted it from the overhead luggage rail he had felt the wound on his arm tear and this caused him to cry out in pain. He thanked the guard and slowly made his way out of the station, his eyes were never too far from the skies and roofs of the station as he ambled across the cobbled street to a waiting taxi cab.

Alistair waited as the taxi driver set down his suitcase near to the wall that surrounded the garden of Olde Tudor. With the fare paid and the taxi now trundling up the hill back towards the centre of Thornbarrow Alistair grimly pushed open the gate and slowly made his way to the front door of the house.

Before he turned the key to unlock the front door he looked around and noted that the snow had practically all melted from the road and surrounding fields, only where it had drifted had it remained as a reminder of the desolation he had felt whilst he had been trapped here not so many days since.

Inside the house Alistair quickly set to work. First, he fitted candles into as many lanterns that he had brought with him. Next, he ensured that both torches were working. He placed a torch in each pocket of his overcoat before he went out the back way towards the workshop.

Alistair tipped the contents from out of two sturdy cardboard boxes. Mostly drill bits, and an assortment of old crockery were spilled out onto the large workbench. He picked up a pair of garden shears and carried the two boxes out of the workshop.

The shears were used to cut through the cords that he and Mortimer had used the bind the gate to the cavern. There were so many knots in the ties it was quicker to sever them than spend the time it would take to untie each knot.

The gate swung inwards. Alistair stood and looked into the dark orifice of the cavern. The hairs on his neck prickled, his heart began to pound in his chest. He wished he could simply turn and run far away and never come back, but he knew if he did then he would never be safe. The phantom, whatever it was came for him the previous night. It would keep on coming for him, attacking him, scraping his flesh until he no longer had any flesh. He would end his life like Smokey, who had been skinned alive.

The wind began to pick up throwing the gate back and forth, it clashed against Alistair's injured leg causing him to flinch with pain. He removed a torch from his pocket and pressed the red stud button near the head of the silver tube. The light was weak in the strong sunlight but when he pointed it into the entrance of the cave it cut a beam through the swirling dust that was caught in the breath of the wind. He collected the two boxes and entered the cave.

The walk to the main chamber did not take him too long. The further away he moved from the exit the darker it became. The light from his torch was clean and bright and he was thankful that Gwen owned such a thing and pondered as to what purpose she used it for.

The beam of light eventually picked out the cave art that dressed the walls at the back of the chamber. Three sets of stencilled hands. The three burial mounds constructed from rocks sat equidistant on the floor below.

He looked about the cavern shining the torch left and right before he approached the burial mounds. He was happy to see he was alone, but his heart was still beating ferociously. He feared he may suffer a cardiac arrest before he was done, and that prospect of ending his days in this dark sepulchre was more horrible than any other idea he had previously carried regarding his own eventual interment.

Alistair set about dismantling the first mound of rocks, shifting the smaller stones that sealed the end of the mound. It was difficult to kneel for such a long time due to pain he felt in his legs, but he continued to work and eventually he had exposed the bones within. He dragged out each and every bone, placing them inside one of the cardboard boxes. He moved on to the second mound and set about removing the seal at the front in the same way as the previous mound.

Once he had exposed the second set of bones he filled up the first box and started to place the remaining bones into the second box, noting that all Redgrave's labels were still present, he could sort the bones later at the house into the respective individual skeletons, he didn't have to be so careful here. He wanted to finish the job as quickly as he could.

As with the first mound, the last pieces to be removed were the skull and neck bones, not wanting to look at the skulls he quickly boxed them. With two mounds emptied he moved on to the third and smaller mound.

The third mound contained smaller bones, this was the child's skeleton he thought as he boxed the pieces finishing with the skull. After he had finished he shone the torch into each mount to ensure he had not missed anything, he certainly did not to have to repeat this task. Happy that he had managed to collect all the bones he got to his feet then wondered how he was going to carry two boxes as well as the torch out of the cavern.

Resting the torch on the first burial mound he stacked one box on top of another and lifted them. It was not such a heavy task but his arm stung as he tried to hold on to them. He placed both boxes back down and recovered the torch. He placed the end of the torch into his mouth and gripped the tube with his teeth. He then bent down and lifted both boxes again. Happy that he had found a solution he was about to leave when he saw what the torchlight was now revealing.

Each set of stencilled hand prints overlooking the graves had somehow started to run and drip down the walls of the cavern. The substance used to create them looked as though it had only been applied seconds ago instead of millennia past. The prints were almost indiscernible as hands now, instead, they had become large blobs of pigment with long trails below, growing longer as they began to resemble Portuguese man o' war jellyfish.

Alistair alarmed by the changing wall art turned and hobbled back out of the chamber and along the cavern passage. He kept moving, gripping the torch between his teeth until his jaws ached. He saw the sunlight greet him at the exit of the cave and snorted with joy at the prospect of leaving and having accomplished his mission.

He left the cave and stumbled through the gate, the wind was constantly pushing the gate into him as though trying to prevent him from leaving its boundary. He spat out the torch and continued to hobble back towards the house, his arm was burning with pain but he clung onto the boxes and finally set them down to rest on the kitchen table before locking the back door.

It took him almost two hours to sort the bones into three separate piles of three individuals. The child's skeleton was the easiest due to the size difference, but he was thankful for Redgrave's labelling for the two adult skeletons. The task was long because of the multitude of separate pieces and the small, almost illegible labels, but now the job was finished.

Each complete adult skeleton was placed into a separate bedsheet and knotted to prevent anything becoming loose. The child skeleton was placed into a pillowcase and similarly knotted.

Alistair intended to carry the bundles all the way up and into town, to St. Peter's church. He decided that he would not contact the reverend Mortimer for any assistance, he didn't want to involve him in any more of this grim business. It would be a long hike to and from the church especially as he needed a spade and he didn't have his bicycle.

Alistair rolled up his shirt sleeve to examine the dressing around his arm. The dark blood stain looked old and there was no sign of any more recent leakage. He glanced at his wristwatch. It was almost three o'clock. A further glance out of the window told him that it would soon be dark, the sun was low in the sky and it had only just turned February. He had to get going. Suddenly a rapping on his front door startled him causing him to jolt.

Standing on the doorstep was the reverend Mortimer. They greeted one another. Alistair invited him inside. Mortimer studied the three bundles arranged on the kitchen floor, "how are you old chap? feeling any better?" Alistair nodded,

"Yes, fine. A couple of days at my sister's house did me the world of good." Mortimer looked at him sceptically,

"I had a call from your sister about an hour ago."

"Gwen? Is there anything wrong, with Gwen I mean?"

"No. She sounded perfectly fine. It was you she was worried about. She called me because you left her with my number, you told her I was a friend of yours," Mortimer smiled, "I'm glad you think so," he added.

"What did Gwen say?"

"She said you'd had a bit of a rum do whilst staying with her. You managed to injure yourself. She thought you could do with some help with a task you'd set out to complete here, well, after the trouble last time I thought it best to check you were indeed alright." Alistair rubbed at his arm lightly then sat down at the kitchen table. He realised there was no point in lying to Mortimer, not at this stage.

"I know you find it difficult to believe the things I told you about, but it came for me. It followed me to Gwen's house." Mortimer stood aghast, then sat down next to Alistair.

"You mean the creature you told me about, the one from the cavern? You are telling me that it followed you all the way to your sister's house?"

"Yes. So, you see John, I must find a way. I must find a way to rid myself of it. I fear for my life, my very soul if I cannot."

"What do you intend to do?"

"I am going to bury the bones at Saint Peter, just like Redgrave intended. Will you help me John?" Alistair suddenly felt tired and weak. He was so fearful for his life and it was only just dawning on him that the task he had set out for himself may well be too much in his current state. It was going to be dark in a couple of hours, the prospect of spending another night alone in this house terrified him, especially now that it contained the remains of what was possibly now haunting him. Gwen was right, he needed help.

Mortimer studied Alistair, the man was almost broken. He had seen the same expression on the face of his predecessor, Redgrave. There was no point in trying to talk sense to him now.

"Of course. What do you need me to do?" Mortimer said. Alistair smiled in relief,

"can we take these skeletons up to the church in your car? I have a spade, I may need help digging the holes, my injuries, you see–"

"I understand. I also have a set of spades in a shed in the churchyard. If we set out now we should be done before dark."

8

Both Mortimer and Alistair were digging holes directly below the three stone tablets. Each etched with Roman numerals. Redgrave's stones. They had completed the first two and were both busy working on the third.

Although only six o'clock, the night had tiptoed in and the moon was shrouded by cloud. Both men worked away by the light produced from two sturdy lanterns, each housing a flickering candle. Alistair had to stop digging; his arm was burning. Mortimer noticed and gestured for him to rest, "I can finish this one, we are almost done. This is not light work my friend, remind me to review the salary the church pays its regular gravediggers, those who prepare the ground for the last farewell!" said Mortimer as he stopped briefly to wipe his brow with a handkerchief. Mortimer continued digging.

Finally, when all three holes were dug, both Mortimer and Alistair went back to the church to fetch the bundles of bones they placed inside before they began the ground work. They each carried a bundle back to the freshly dug graves with Mortimer returning for the final heap. With all three skeletons at the graveside, they tipped each sack into a separate hole, "and now the heavy work continues as we cover them over," said Mortimer, handing Alistair a spade.

It took them a further hour to fill in all the holes with dirt standing proud over each grave. Using the backs of the spades they flattened down and packed the dirt flat. They both stood in silence for a moment as though they had just conducted a burial of a dearly departed loved one. "Do you think we should say something, I mean it is a burial, isn't it?" Alistair said looking at Mortimer for help finding some words to utter. Mortimer cleared his throat,

"for we know that if the earthly tent we live in is destroyed, we have a building from God. A house not made with hands, and eternal in the heavens," Mortimer finished. Alistair nodded to say that the words were well chosen. They each took up a lantern and made their way back to the church.

The church was illuminated by a multitude of hanging lamps as they both washed in separate vestibules that contained a sink and toilet. When they had finished cleaning up they met in the nave. "All that work has made me ravenous, you too I shouldn't wonder," spoke Mortimer, "I have some bread, cake, and cheese in the small kitchen behind the narthex. I dare say I would even be able to put my hand on a bottle of wine!"

"Yes, thank you, I am rather hungry. And to be honest, relieved I have done what I knew I had to do," answered Alistair as he slid himself down onto a pew.

"I shall fetch us a bite to eat, shan't be long." Mortimer disappeared behind an elaborately carved screen filled with cherubs and angels.

Alistair rolled up his trousers to check on his wounds. The right leg thigh looked unchanged, however his calf bandage was moist with new blood. He rolled his trouser leg back down, at least now he could aim to seek medical attention for his wounds. He intended to go to the hospital at Suffield Park, Cromer, the following day once he had returned to Gwen's house.

To Alistair's delight, Mortimer returned carrying a tray of much needed refreshment, and true to his word he brought a bottle of wine. Both men chatted as they ate, Alistair spoke about his plans to sell Olde Tudor and live near Gwen. Mortimer spoke about new plans to repair parts of the church that had been damaged during the war. When they finished their meal, Mortimer invited Alistair to stop at the vicarage rather than to return back to Olde Tudor, "your offer is very kind John, but I have one more favour to ask,"

"Name it."

"I should very much like to stay here for the night, at Saint Peter," said Alistair. Mortimer looked a little shocked,

"Stay here? Why would you want to do that?"

"I feel safe here, protected. It's a holy place, a godly place, nothing like that cavern. I would be too nervous to stop anywhere else, especially after last night at Gwen's. Could I be allowed to stop here do you think?" Mortimer downed his last drop of wine,

"If that's what you want, but I find it a little odd. I would have to lock you in you understand. There are many vagrants around these parts who would love to get their hands on a couple of gold plated candlesticks. I'm all for helping the poor but church property is church property!"

"Yes, I understand, besides, being locked in makes me feel even more secure. So, if you don't mind . . ."

"If it would make you feel at ease tonight I have no problem with the arrangement," Mortimer said. Once they had cleared away the remains of supper, the reverend said that he would be back first thing in the morning and he locked up the church leaving Alistair alone inside.

Alistair Pulled a couple of pews together, he picked up a roll of blankets that Mortimer had left out for him and laid them on the pews. Then, he took two kneeler cushions and arranged them as a pillow. Not the most comfortable bed he thought, but it will do. Nothing in the world would be able to make him go back to Olde Tudor tonight.

Before he settled in his makeshift bed, Alistair took a stroll around the church nave and beyond. It was a strange experience being alone at night in a church, it was something he had never done before, unless you counted the time he and Evelyn took refuse in the cellar of Saint John's church in Sheffield during one of the air raids. During that fearful night there were other people, other parishioners. He was all alone in Saint Peter.

******

The reverend John Mortimer was early to rise the next morning. He had a quick breakfast of toast and marmalade, and had packed a few items that he thought Alistair would need for breakfast. He took the car to Saint Peter and arrived at eight thirty. When he unlocked the church, he found Alistair busy replacing the pews he had rearranged the night before. They greeted one another and Mortimer was the first to speak, "to be honest I was worried about you being here all alone last night, was everything alright?" Alistair hobbled over to Mortimer stiffly,

"I had a peaceful sleep, a much-needed peaceful sleep. However, my legs and arm are troubling me today, I think I will pay a visit to the hospital as the doctor advised."

"I'm very glad to hear it. Do you need a lift anywhere?"

"I have to go back to Olde Tudor to collect a few things, but a lift to the station would be very handy," replied Alistair hopefully.

"Of course. What time should I call round?" Alistair glanced at his watch, shall we say about ten?"

"Ten it is. Would you like a lift down to the cottage?"

"I think I would like to walk. Clear my head. My legs are a little stiff, but the more I sit around the worse they get."

"Well if you change your mind, I shall be around the church, in my office at the back." Mortimer handed him the breakfast he brought him. Alistair thanked him and tucked into the bread and marmalade greedily.

Alistair knocked politely on the half open office door, he entered to find Mortimer busy at a small desk looking through some papers, there was a fresh pot of tea on the desk. "I wanted to thank you for the breakfast and to say that I'll be making my way back to the cottage." Mortimer stopped his work briefly,

"I shall pick you up at ten as arranged," he said cheerfully.

"Thank you, I hope I haven't been too much of a bother!"

"Not at all, it's the duty of a parish priest to assist one's flock so to speak." Alistair said goodbye then made his way out of the church. He stood briefly to inhale the cool morning air and to enjoy the bright sunshine before moving off along the path that led through the churchyard and out onto the street beyond. There was a lightness to his mood as though a thick heavy cloud had been blown away.

Mortimer filed away the paperwork he had been studying regarding the plans for the rebuilding work at the church. He poured out the last tea from the pot into a cup and decided to take it with him during his regular morning stroll through the churchyard.

Mortimer had only walked a few paces in front of the church when he spotted something that perturbed him. Leaving his teacup to rest on a bench he hurriedly made his way across the lawn that had started sprouting crocus and snowdrop.

Stopping finally at the site of the three stone tablets where he and Alistair had buried the bones the previous night, Mortimer's jaw hung agape as he studied the unbelievable sight before him. The three graves had been dug out, but not it seemed by spade. It was as though they had been clawed out by an animal. A mound of scattered earth lay at the foot of each hole, and in each pit, there were a pile of soil coated rags, the remains of the linen sheets that had once contained all three skeletons.

Alistair had almost made it back to Olde Tudor. He could see the house at the end of the lane. It was then that he heard the call of a raven. Alarmed he looked up and around him wildly until he found the bird perched high on a tree top, some way ahead. Hunched and leering at him.

His gaze also picked out something else beneath the bird at the base of the tree. A form, almost a shadow. The form of a man. The man was wearing the apparel of a vicar, and he was pointing. Warning. And then in the blink of an eye, the man was gone.

Alistair turned to follow the direction to where the shadow had pointed. There was a new figure, this time it was not a shadow, but a solid form striding down the sloping lane. It was coming for him.

The figure was silhouetted with the sun behind it. Alistair noticed its jerky gait, it was not walking properly. There was something odd about this thing that was making a determined line down the lane towards him. Alistair became frightened, forgetting his wounded legs he turned and ran the last few yards to the gate to Olde Tudor.

The catch on the gate became stuck as Alistair rattled and pulled and pushed in his haste to get it open. He then became aware of the sound that the striding thing was making. A grinding, splintering, cracking sound. Alistair turned and looked upon the form of the thing that he realised now had been his tormenter, the cavern dwelling abhorrence.

The thing was an amalgamation of old bones, old bones with labels. It was trying to walk upright but the bones were breaking and splintering as they rubbed together at the joints. The head of the thing, a skull set in a rictus grin, was bobbing up and down like a puppet on a string.

Alistair managed to free the gate and he hobbled through and up the path that led around the back of the house, he dared not turn and look to see if the creature was still in pursuit of him, he didn't have to look. He could hear it coming, the snapping, rubbing, grinding followed him.

Mortimer had finally snapped himself out of his trance at finding the dereliction of the three graves. He raced around the front of the church and climbed into his car. He pulled away at great speed through the churchyard gates almost knocking down an elderly parishioner as she slowly ambled past St. Peter clutching a shopping basket.

Mortimer slammed hard on the brakes, his car came to a screeching stop. The startled elderly woman almost fainted in fright, "I'm terribly sorry, forgive me Mrs Smithson," he shouted before driving away leaving Mrs Smithson clutching at her breast whilst she regained her senses.

Mortimer's black Rover 75 was driven with speed all the way out of Thornbarrow and all the way down to Olde Tudor. Parked outside, Mortimer left the car unlocked and ran up to the front door. He rapped loudly whilst calling for Alistair but got no response.

He made his way around the back of the cottage and rapped on the back door. After several attempts at knocking he tried to force his way in but could not move the door.

The gate to the cavern crashed against its post in the sturdy breeze. Mortimer turned to look, almost out of reflex, then he saw something, or someone, lying face down next to the monolith. Gingerly he approached the form on the ground and inhaled sharply when he recognised the overcoat, it was Alistair.

Mortimer rolled Alistair over then quickly turned away, "Lord, God, no!" he cried. "Why?" he said finally as he forced himself to look again briefly at Alistair's face, or what remained of it. Strips of skin had been removed and his head had been partially scalped. Lying next to Alistair's body was a stone axe. Unbeknown to Mortimer, it was the same axe Alistair had recovered from the workshop. A prehistoric tool the late reverend Redgrave had excavated from the cavern. It was now covered in Alistair's blood.

******

Two weeks following the discovery of the body at Olde Tudor, Mortimer was now conducting the service for Alistair's burial. A few local townsfolk had turned up, the same few who always appeared at every funeral the reverend Mortimer had conducted since starting work at St. Peter.

Gwen was also present, being his only relative she had to organise the funeral. She was being consoled by an old colleague of Alistair's from his school teaching days.

Mortimer had spoken to Gwen before the service had started. He offered his deepest condolences and told her that he was the one who had found him. He didn't tell her about the two of them burying the bones the night before. He felt this was an unnecessary detail she could live without knowing, and it would avoid having to explain the unscheduled activity to members of the parish council if word got out.

Whilst they waited for the coffin to be lowered into the earth, Mortimer spotted two figures standing over by where he and Alistair had buried the bones from the cavern. They were too far away for him to see any features, they both seemed to be standing stiffly as though they were watching the proceedings. He wondered why they didn't come over if they were known to the Swift family. He was about to ask Gwen if she knew who they were but he was stopped by one of the Brierly's who ran the property business in the town. It was

135

Jacob Brierly, "Nasty business Reverend," spoke Jacob,

"Yes, yes indeed."

"And you finding him. Terrible. Do they know what happened? The police I mean?" Mortimer glanced back over to where the two figures had stood moments ago, they were both gone. "Burglar I expect. Is that it?"

"What, oh, yes, I expect that's probably what it was. Poor chap," finished Mortimer.

"I shall have to have a word with his wife afterwards, with her inheriting the house," Jacob added,

"Wife? Oh, you mean Gwen, no she's his sister, but as far as I know he didn't have any other family," said Mortimer thoughtfully.

"Well looks like she's just inherited Olde Tudor, her brother recently put it back on the market. I will have to find out if she intends to continue with a sale," Jacob finished and he moved away to stand near to Gwen. Mortimer scanned the churchyard for another sight of the two strangers but saw nothing.

With the funeral party all leaving to attend the wake that was being held in the local inn, Mortimer collected his service book and left the gravediggers to fill in the hole. He walked over to the three stone tablets, where he saw the two figures earlier, "I believe you," he spoke softly as he thought about Redgrave and Alistair.

As Mortimer turned to leave for the church, a raven dived down from a nearby rowan tree and attacked him, scoring a red line down his cheek.

"The damnedest thing!" he exclaimed and took a handkerchief from his pocket to dab at the wound. He quickened his pace and made for the church.

Inside one of the vestibules he rinsed his reddened handkerchief under a tap and tried to clean the wound. He stopped rubbing when he heard a sound like a laboured breathing. He turned the tap to stop the flow of water so he could listen for the sound again. It came once more. Mortimer dropped the handkerchief and raised his hands to his mouth to stop his jaw trembling. He was now very afraid.

The Author would appreciate a written review on Amazon.

Have you also read:

The Mermaid's Ring
Book of doors – The Golden Prince
Songs in the graveyard
Icy Creeps – Gothic Tales of Terror
The Paranatural Detective Agency Volume 1 & 2

For information on the above titles by the same author visit:
http://davidralphwilliams.webs.com

Printed in Great Britain
by Amazon